Newport Dreams

· · · · · · · · · ·

Also by Shelley Noble

NEWPORT DREAMS

. . . .

A Breakwater Bay Novella

SHELLEY NOBLE

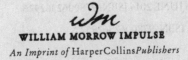

WILLIAM MORROW IMPULSE

An Imprint of HarperCollinsPublishers

EPub Edition JUNE 2014 ISBN: 9780062362926

Print Edition ISBN: 9780062362957

10 9 8 7 6 5

Chapter 1

. . . .

THE PLACE WAS a disaster. It had to be the ugliest, most neglected house in Newport. But this was her last chance. Get a job that you can keep or lose your allowance. It was a stupid spot to be in. She was twenty-four, had studied at three colleges, traveled the world, hung out with the rich and famous; she really shouldn't need an allowance. Unfortunately she hadn't learned to live without it.

Now this neglected eyesore would decide whether she would continue to live in the style to which she'd always been accustomed or admit failure and give in to the pressures of her corporate-minded family.

Geordie Holt sneaked a peek at her new colleagues. They were oohing and aahing over the dilapidated house as if they were witnessing the unveiling of the Breakers, the Vanderbilt mansion on Bellevue Avenue that set the standard for the Gilded Age architecture.

There was no way this would ever look like anything but what it was: an abandoned boardinghouse. Shingles were missing, the porch sagged, the front steps were crumbling, half the windows were boarded over and there wasn't enough glass in the others to keep the rain out of one.

And paint? Missing in action, except for a few flakes of baby-poop beige that had fallen to the ground, revealing even uglier baby-poop brown. Her camera equipment suddenly felt very heavy.

"So what do you think?" Doug Paxton, hands stuffed in the pockets of his jeans, frowned up at the facade. He was project manager, a little older than the rest of the group— maybe late thirties—and had to be wondering why he ever pitched this project to this board of directors.

"Fantastic," said the woman next to him. She was dark haired and beautiful in a neo Raphaelite way. She'd introduced herself earlier as Mary. Geordie knew from the contact sheet that it was spelled *Meri*. She wondered what the story behind that was. Her fingers were itching to photograph Meri just like she was right now, totally fascinated with something that only she could see.

Though Doug was a close second. He let out a breath and began talking to the architect on the project, Bruce Stafford. Geordie had googled them all as soon as she was hired. But Bruce was the one who had caught her eye. He was tallish, darkish, and hottish. The kind of guy who looked like he'd be safe to pick up in a bar. Not that she was doing that these days. But she did look twice.

"Can we get inside?" Meri asked.

"Sure," Bruce said. "It's been inspected and it's structurally sound but needs some repairs before it's totally safe. Just watch out for loose handrails. And rotten floorboards. I had the inspector mark any places that he thought might be dangerous. Just stick with the group until we've done a full recce."

Doug moved to the side. He walked with a noticeable limp. "Let's give Geordie a minute to take some establishing shots."

"Good idea." Bruce Stafford smiled at her almost as if he could see what a fake she was.

"Of course." Geordie knew what she was supposed to do. She'd spent three sleep-deprived evenings at the RISD library reading everything she could find about architectural photography, cramming for her interview at the historical society.

And she'd actually pulled it off.

Now she understood why. Who in their right mind would want this job?

"Do you have a wide-angle lens? Or do you want to set up across the street?"

She gave the smug architect a smile to match his own. "Both."

She lugged her cameras and tripod out to the pavement. Looked up at the house, checked the sun and moved farther out into the street, just as a car turned the corner and swerved out of her way.

Ugh. She was making a great impression. She chose a spot between two parked cars and began setting up her tripod. She'd always taken photos. She'd even taken three semesters of photography in college, but couldn't convince her family that it could be a real profession.

She interned with a fashion photographer. A few days among those highly stressed, anorexic, insecure models, makeup people, designers, and hair stylists . . . even the photographer . . . well, that was enough for her.

She normally was good at photographing people. But there she never could get past the "editorial" look.

This job sounded perfect. Calm, artistic, and civilized. Creative.

So much for truth in advertising.

There was no way this eyesore would ever come close to the real Newport mansions. It had "Restoration Impossible" written all over it.

But she needed this job. She only hoped it would last.

She set up her camera and waited for another car to pass. Took a couple of candid shots of the group then motioned them to move out of frame. Took several color and black-and-whites of the front facade. Zoomed in for a few close-ups. And just for the hell of it she shifted the camera and caught the glint of stained glass between two branches of an old sprawling tree, oak or something. Took a quick look at the shot she'd captured. Nice.

"Hey, are you finished yet?"

She nodded and capped the lens, put the cameras over her shoulder, folded up the tripod.

She really needed to remember that she was here for documentation. Not to be creative. Stay focused and not be distracted by shiny things, like the fragments of color framed by a tracery of branches. The place where the patch on Doug's jacket was coming unstitched. The look on Meri's face as she gazed up at something that Geordie couldn't see—or how the light lifted the Titian highlights of her hair. The fun things.

You're not here to have fun.

Bruce motioned impatiently to her. "I need you to get a close-up of the front steps." He turned to Doug and Meri. "I'm thinking under that paint is some glass tile inlay. Hard to tell in this light, but last night with a flashlight, there's a definite pattern of something under that . . ." Bruce waved his hand dismissing what Geordie would call medium-mildew-green paint that covered the steps and the sides in thick layers and was probably the only thing keeping the concrete from disintegrating.

She got as close as she safely could. Looked for any signs of inlay. The architect had better eyes than she did. Then she saw it, the slightest indentation in the paint. Not even full lines but a sort of dit and dot occurrence that formed a vague pattern.

Wow. Geordie was impressed that he'd found it. She could appreciate a good eye, even if it belonged to a grouch.

She took a few shots of the steps. Moved closer to get more detail.

A large hand gripped her arm and pulled her back. "I said not too close." He was staring at her and he didn't let go. She tried to ease her arm out of his fingers to no avail.

"I know what I'm doing," she said, returning his stare.

A long moment passed, some kind of standoff that Geordie didn't quite understand. Finally he said, "Do you?" and dropped her arm. She moved out of range and joined the others who were talking animatedly about something on the side of the house and hadn't seen his odd behavior.

She spent the next few minutes taking closer views of the house's facade. She tried not to look for unusual shots—just get what she was being paid to get. And tried to forget the intensity of Bruce Stafford's hold. More anger, she thought, than a desire to keep her from injury.

"Okay, that's enough." Bruce again. They called Doug "Boss," but Bruce was throwing around the orders. Maybe because Doug and Meri were busy talking and gesticulating at each other. Some words Geordie recognized. She'd taken an Intro to Architecture class and visited the Newport mansions more times than she could count, mainly to study the pictures of the people who had lived in them. Wondered what they were really like.

"We have to go in the back," Bruce said to the others. "The front steps are ready to fall."

Meri and Doug started toward the back of the house and the parking lot without missing a beat of their conversation.

Geordie waited for the angry architect to follow them before falling into step with the one other person in the group, Carlyn, a redhead who had her nose buried in her iPad and incongruously had a mechanical pencil stuck behind her ear. She hadn't said a word since her first hello, just kept typing and saving.

The back steps were wood and looked worse than the front ones.

"Stay close to the stringers. The wood is weakened." Bruce

turned to Geordie. "Don't bother with these. They are a later addition and have to be replaced."

She nodded and followed the others single file along the left side of the stairs.

As they reached the back door, Geordie could feel the shift in the group's energy. Until now, they had been thrumming with anticipation. Doug unlocked the door and that energy burst into space.

Geordie had felt that energy in her own work.

They all crowded inside, leaving her behind to juggle two cameras, a bag of lenses and a tripod through the door.

She was immediately swallowed by darkness. She could hear the others up ahead, and she stumbled after them, camera equipment banging against her side. Gradually a rectangle of lighter darkness appeared. Geordie groped her way into what appeared to be a kitchen.

A camp lantern had been set in the middle of a wobbly rectangular table. There were no chairs. The linoleum that covered the floor was cracked and missing altogether in places.

Meri turned around. "Sorry. Didn't mean to leave you behind. We're all so used to working together, we just tend to migrate to a home base." She reached for the tripod and Geordie handed it over. She had a sudden urge to shove the cameras at her and make a run for it, but the architect stood in the doorway, blocking her escape.

She forced a smile. "Thanks."

"Just say when you need something. You'll adjust. It always takes a few days on a new project. Especially when you haven't worked with the crew before. Don't be shy."

Shy? Geordie prided herself on never appearing shy. She wasn't. Exactly. More like ... insecure. Okay, there it was. She was insecure. All the time. It was because she had no purpose in life. It had to be that. Because she was smart ... enough. Pretty ... more than enough if she did say so herself. Had money so she never had to sponge off her friends and she was good for a loan. People generally liked her—at least until they found out she had no plan for her life.

"Electricity should be on by tomorrow," Doug said. "I thought this would be good enough for a base camp until we decide how we want to work. Carlyn, there are several small rooms, probably once a bedroom that's been partitioned into storage areas. Two have windows. They might do for offices and there's another room, a later addition, I thought would do for supplies and equipment."

Carlyn merely nodded and kept typing.

Doug slipped out of a backpack that he'd had on since they'd arrived and pulled out a metal tube. He wiped the table off with the arm of his jacket, popped off one end of the tube and slid a rolled paper onto the table.

Everyone crowded around. Geordie hesitated, not knowing if she was supposed to look or to mind her own business. They all seemed to mesh like a well-oiled machine.

Meri glanced back at her and moved over to make room. Geordie put her equipment on the counter and squeezed in between Carlyn and Meri.

It was a blueprint of the house. It looked much bigger than Geordie had expected. Bruce began to explain things, drawing arrows, circles and x's in pencil. Doug added his marks to Bruce's and before long the print was completely decorated. He and Doug had evidently been in before, had enough ideas for everybody and hopefully had more than one copy of the blueprint.

As they passed ideas and opinions around, Carlyn continued to take notes, and Geordie's mind began to wander.

The kitchen wasn't so bad. Old and beat up. But the cabinets were real wood as far as she could tell. They were painted over with some seventies avocado kitchen green, but . . . She wandered over and opened one of the doors. Something skittered away and she bit back a yelp and slammed the door.

Bruce looked up from where they were still bent over the plans and shook his head. "Exterminator will be in next week sometime. It won't get rid of all the creepy crawlies, they've been here long enough to call it home, so if you're squeamish—"

"I'm not."

"Huh." He went back to listening to Doug.

She wandered back to see what held them enthralled.

A few minutes later Doug was leading them on a tour of the house. A long hallway with wallpaper peeling on each side led to the projected offices and storeroom. No one said anything to Geordie, not even to give her instructions, so she snapped photos as she went, just to make herself feel like she had a reason to be there.

She assumed she would come back for more detailed work once they got lights and cleared out some of the garbage, of which there was plenty. Old newspapers were stacked up in corners, a mildewed rug was rolled up across a doorway. There was dust everywhere and so thick that they left footprints wherever they went.

And the smell. Geordie had to fight not to cover her nose. The others seemed oblivious, until Carlyn stopped.

"Doug, you know there's only one thing I won't do for you."

Doug laughed. "I know. It is pretty ripe. I'll bring in a crew to clean up before you have to set up."

Carlyn grinned. "Thank you. Uh-oh, she's found something."

They'd reached the end of the hall. To their left was a staircase to the second floor and a hallway that led to the back of the house. To their right was a two-storied foyer, and in the middle Meri stood, feet planted, head thrown back looking at the ceiling.

Geordie got off a quick succession of shots of Meri's back before they all looked up.

There was a big reproduction Early American-style chandelier dead center. A style Geordie knew had never been popular in Newport, Rhode Island, even the first time around. Cracks radiated from the medallion, also a repro, that held it to the ceiling. The ceiling was painted dark blue, or green—it was hard to tell. In places where the painter had totally missed with the paintbrush, a dirty shade of goldenrod showed through the blue—or green.

Just looking at it made her head spin.

She snapped her head down and concentrated on studying the walls. The whole house looked as if it had been painted during the "Early Psychedelic" period—neon oranges, yellows, blues.

The room at least was interesting, octagon shaped with wainscoting that reached halfway up the wall. The door that had been boarded over from the outside was dark oak with a transept window still intact and made up of hundreds of pieces of stained glass.

"Oh yeah," Meri said. She sounded like she had just struck the mother lode. "How soon can we get scaffolding set up?"

Scaffolding? Geordie's breath caught. No one had said anything about scaffolding.

Doug laughed. "Next week, hopefully. There's a lot more to do before we start work."

"I know but . . ."

You'd think it was Christmas they way they were talking. Geordie forced herself to take a quick look up at the ceiling. "Should I take a photo?"

"Yes, and a few of the transom for now," Bruce said. "And any other place that is fragile enough that it might be damaged in the cleanup."

She could do that. She moved away from the others and soon became lost in taking pictures of all sorts of things. Woodwork that had been chewed by some rodent or hungry hippie, water damage on a patterned wallpaper that had curled at the edges and revealed the promise of a more intriguing paper underneath.

She pulled back one of the edges.

"Please, do not touch anything. We have experts for that."

Geordie spun around, not that she hadn't already learned to recognize that voice. Bruce Stafford looked annoyed.

"Sorry. I just wanted to see what was underneath."

"You and the rest of the world. You can't rush into these things. It must be done slowly, carefully, and methodically. By experts."

And he clearly thought she wasn't one of them.

He gave her a long penetrating look and she took a photo of him just to be annoying.

He raised one eyebrow. "Don't get separated from the others."

Geordie was tempted to take another shot, but he turned and walked away. And all she could do was watch and fume and try to control the blush that had traveled up her neck and spread across her face.

Chapter 2

· · · · · · · · · ·

"I THOUGHT YOU said you were hiring a photographer." Bruce paced along the narrow space between the kitchen sink and table. "Instead we get an intern who can't stay focused or follow orders, and takes pictures like she was a tourist. If she's even studied architecture I'll be amazed. I hope to hell we're not paying her."

Doug was one of the best project managers in Newport. Bruce always tried to work with him. Before he'd crashed through a supposedly inspected floor to the marble of the floor below, he'd been one of the best restorers in town. He knew the business and the people in it and he didn't usually make these kinds of mistakes. What the hell had he been thinking to hire Geordie Holt?

Meri glanced from Doug to Bruce. "She seemed okay to me. She got lots of shots."

"Yeah, but of what? I caught her doing multiple close-ups

of curling wallpaper. And not in a way that could possibly be useful. What the hell is that about? Didn't the grant request go through?"

"Yeah, it did," Doug said. "And she isn't an intern."

Bruce stopped pacing and turned to face the project manager. "A volunteer?"

Doug shook his head.

Bruce got a terrible sinking feeling. "She's a professional?"

Doug nodded.

"You saw her credentials?"

"I saw her portfolio. The woman takes a good photo."

"This doesn't sound like you."

"Look, Bruce. No one I like working with was available, which was just as well, since she was part of the bargain."

Bruce pulled out a chair and sat down. A really terrible feeling. "Let me guess, somebody's niece, granddaughter, or spoiled daughter and who contributes to the board. I knew it."

"Maybe. She applied, we hired her. There wasn't a lot of choice out there. And I had to cut some corners."

"Which you'd know if you didn't have your head in the restoration clouds." Carlyn said. She was slightly flushed. "Geordie Holt isn't the only one who isn't focused on the here and now."

Doug grinned at her. "That's what we have you for. To keep us on the straight and narrow." Carlyn was the financial whiz kid, accountant, development coordinator, publicist, marketer, lunchtime gopher and whatever else came her way. She was devoted to Doug. And best friends with Meri.

"So they held you hostage until you hired her?"

"We're not paying her, the board is."

"What? Never heard of such a thing."

"Well, I think we should wait until she uploads her photos before we judge," Meri said.

"So we're stuck with her?"

Doug shrugged. "Pretty much."

"What a couple of jaded old grumps. Maybe it's her first project. She's probably nervous and you didn't exactly make her feel welcome. She was practically quaking when she left."

Bruce glowered at her. "I was nice."

"As ice," Carlyn said under breath. "You just don't like her because she drives a fancy sports car."

"It's not about cars, it's about expertise."

Meri rolled her eyes and stood. "I'm going to check out my ceiling. Give her time to settle down. Don't worry. We got the grant and if we have to do a little extra until she gets up to speed . . . Doug and I know our way around a camera. We do most of our own documentation anyway. Cheaper that way." Meri headed to the door.

"Be careful out there," Doug said.

"Aye, Aye, Captain," Meri saluted and disappeared.

"Guess I'll go chose small or smaller for an office so I can start moving my equipment in."

"Carlyn," Doug began.

"I know, be careful. Have I ever not been?" She headed to the door.

"So what do you really think?" Bruce asked as he sat down across from Doug.

"I think you're too stressed out over this photographer and this project. We haven't even started yet."

Bruce sighed. He knew he was. He was taking on way more work than he had time for just so he could make enough real money to moonlight on independent projects like Gilbert House.

It was a diamond in the rough. He had a feeling about it. So did Doug. And Doug didn't miss much. When he'd called Bruce to tell him he'd found a hidden wonder, Bruce didn't hesitate to say yes. And once he'd seen the building for himself, he was hooked. Even before he'd run the inspections to make sure it was recoverable, he was totally committed.

That's what he liked about Doug and his team of restorers. They were a practiced crew with a master at the helm. That's what was so infuriating about this photographer.

Everybody had to carry their weight and more. Had to wear several hats at once, and be willing to work for little remuneration. Geordie Holt with her designer jeans and manicured nails was fluff. And none of them had time for fluff.

BRUCE WALKED HOME, hands in his pockets and his head in a quandary. He should be happy. Gilbert House had good bones. But he wasn't.

He stopped at the deli, looked at his reflection in the glass door before going inside. It was that girl, woman, the photographer, Geordie Holt.

He opened the door and went inside.

His reaction to her had been over the top. She had an attitude, but creative people sometimes did. And she was creative, if the way she crawled around taking shots of stuff they would never need was any indication. But they didn't need creative, they just needed meticulous documentation.

At least she seemed to be into details. Too much so, he thought, as he remembered her taking several close-ups of a windowsill from various angles. Not to mention candid shots of the crew. What was with that? He'd asked her what she was doing.

She'd ignored him. Or maybe she hadn't even heard him. Maybe she had some kind of Asperger's.

She obviously knew her photography but it was equally obvious that she was inexperienced in the field of restoration photography. Of course they dealt with inexperience all the time; when you worked on a shoestring budget you took on a lot of interns and volunteers.

She was also obviously rich and spoiled, by the looks of her clothes and all that equipment. And that attitude. That wasn't what bothered him. Actually it wasn't her at all. She just happened to be the most recent annoyance in a string of annoyances.

Geordie Holt wasn't really the problem. It wasn't her fault that she had the things he wanted, was the kind of woman that interested him. And as far from his reach as possible. The truth was he was barely making it.

He ordered his usual evening meal, sandwich and salad, grabbed a newspaper and continued on his way.

He'd been so sure of himself when he'd picked up and left the architectural firm to strike out on his own. He thought that being his own boss would give him more time to do more restoration work. Gradually build a reputation so he would be able to segue into full-time restoration.

Just as soon as he paid off all those student loans.

It had taken him a good six years to work and borrow his way through college. Maybe he should have stuck it out in a larger firm for a few more years, but he'd been impatient.

So far he'd been pretty successful on his own. He had more work than he could handle. Plenty of clients. Unfortunately quite a few never paid him on time.

He climbed the steps to his house, grabbed a beer from the fridge and sat down at his computer to eat his dinner and catch up on the paying work he'd let slide while spending the day on a recce at Gilbert House.

When Doug called a few weeks before, waxing enthusiastic over a house he'd found and looking for a consultant he could trust and who worked cheap, Bruce couldn't say no. It hadn't even occurred to him to say no.

How could he? Doug had a genius for finding teardowns and turning them into showplaces. One look at Gilbert House, and Bruce knew Doug had done it again.

It was a mess. Would take loads of work, a knowledgeable crew. More money. Daunting, but Bruce had confidence in Doug. And he could see Gilbert House's future in his mind, as clearly as if he was looking at a color photo of the finished product.

The idea of which pissed him off all over again. They could have brought in an unpaid intern and used Geordie Holt's salary for more pressing needs.

Sandwich forgotten, he tugged on his beer and looked down at the plans on his drafting table. Not plans for Gilbert House, but a renovation of a townhouse bathroom, marble tub and vanity. Tumbled tile floor. There was nothing wrong with the bathroom they had now, but they had to have the very best and newest fad. The damn place was only ten years old. But at least they paid on time.

He looked around his own house. It had plenty of period detail and was in need of some major TLC. But it would have to wait. It always had to wait. He'd managed to gut the kitchen and bathroom, thinking that once those two were finished he could tackle everything else piecemeal. But the plumbing sucked, had to be completely changed out.

Now the plumbing was fixed but he'd spent way too much money—and time. He'd had to keep the old appliances and leave the linoleum floor instead of reclaiming the old flooring. So now he worked late every night and on weekends, subsisting on deli food and frozen dinners heated in the microwave.

Hell, his house wasn't in much better shape than Gilbert house. And the heat? Nonexistent. That would be another money suck. But it would have to be remedied. Winter was just a couple of months away.

GEORDIE SAT AT her desk spotlighted by the glow from four computer screens that filled the dining niche of her apartment. She had state-of-the-art equipment and she thanked her lucky stars that she'd bought it while her family was still supplying her every whim. It gave her a cutting edge in the business, whatever that business turned out to be.

But she was beginning to see that having things made easy by her family had made her ill equipped to take care of herself. Hell, this apartment wasn't even hers, just a pied-à-terre her family kept for visiting clients.

And now their wayward daughter.

Well, what was she supposed to do until she saved some money and could make it on her own? Maybe that was the problem. She didn't have to make it on her own.

Her family was rich. Had indulged her every whim. They'd indulged her sisters, too, but they had lived up to the family expectations, had respectable careers, married well.

But not Geordie. Even as a child she could never settle for one thing. Always felt different. She was different. Had never quite measured up. Now she had to show them that all their indulgence had been worthwhile. That she was worthwhile.

And that same feeling of panic set in, the need to get out, go somewhere, anywhere that captured her imagination, kept her busy. Find a place that said *Stay here, this is where you belong.*

It wasn't like she hadn't been looking. She'd been desperate to find something that would show that she was a mature adult and didn't have to be scolded every time something didn't turn out the way she'd expected.

Like being a fashion photographer. She loved photography. Some of her best shots were of people. But models posed, did what they were told to do. Some of them transcended the genre. But for the most part, Geordie had found that their facades and their "looks" were already finely honed, strong. And trying to cut through all that sleekness to reach something essential was too exhausting.

She had taken some good shots. But her best shots were caught when the models had finished, were tired. Leaning over to take off a shoe or sitting before a makeup table with no makeup. Of course those were unusable. But for Geordie, that's where photography belonged. When the subject was unsuspecting. Caught when all the external stuff was forgotten, in a moment of indecision, anger, introspection, fatigue. Moments like that gave you a window to a person's soul.

Without them even knowing it.

People face-to-face made her nervous. That was obvious this morning when she'd blundered into her latest fiasco with enthusiasm and intensity only to flounder and embarrass herself.

The architect hated her, thought she was a flake and clueless. And what made it worse, was he was probably right. She'd taken hundreds of photos on-site, but most of them would be totally unusable for what the team needed.

She swiveled her chair from her large graphics monitor to a smaller one. Several rows of thumbnail-size photos stared back at her. More than could fit on the screen. She'd taken more than a hundred shots today and as she looked them over, she realized she might not have taken enough.

Okay, not enough of what she was supposed to look at. But she'd just followed her eye. At a certain level the house was fascinating. All that light and dark play through shuttered windows. *Like this one.* She clicked on it and an enlarged photo appeared.

A perfect triangular dash of sunlight, its point pricking the dark oak windowsill like a shard of glass, unleashing the life of the wood and sending the grain racing away from the point. And the one she'd caught immediately after, as Carlyn stepped into the same light and a halo appeared around her curly hair. And the two together . . .

She opened the photo in her graphics program and spent the next few minutes enhancing and clarifying and playing with the contrasts, overlaying and editing, fragmenting and enhancing—until she remembered that she was supposed to be organizing her documentation of the day's work.

She pulled her eye from the computer screen, checked the time, and realized that it had been more then a few minutes; she'd been playing with that same photograph for more than an hour.

She saved the work and clicked out of it. Returned her attention to her rows of photos and began to organize them according to subject matter and time of day.

After two hours her eyes were burning, her back was aching, and her stomach was growling, but she had twenty different files of architectural details.

She looked over the files, wondering if there were too many. That was one thing she hadn't been able to learn: how to organize the files in a useful way rather than a creative way. To recognize what was wanted and what was superfluous. Well, she could learn.

She stood up. Stretched, touched her toes and hung there until her back stopped hurting, then walked across the wooden floor to the balcony doors. She opened one and stood just inside the threshold and let the cool air energize her.

In the distance, lights were blinking around the harbor. She was hungry. She could go out, but she hated eating alone—almost as much as she hated sleeping alone in the sleek king-sized bed in the next room.

This was no ordinary pied-à-terre. It was a huge loft in one of the harbor buildings downtown. White walls, open space, big and clean enough to be an art gallery. Perfect for her enlarged and mounted photos that were lined up against the wall on the floor. God forbid she stuck a nail in those pristine walls.

She slid the door closed, walked back past her belongings piled in one corner and went to the kitchen, carefully avoiding the mail and the envelope that had arrived that morning on schedule just as it did every month. Anytime now, the phone call would follow.

"Did you get the check?"

"Yes, Dad. Thank you."

"How's the job hunt coming?"

"Fine."

"You know there's a place—"

"I know."

He'd grunt. They'd say good-bye and wait another month to have the same conversation when her next allowance check arrived.

The fridge was stocked with the usual: pâté, gourmet cheese, bottled designer water, two bottles of Moët champagne. Plenty of ice in the freezer for the stocked liquor cabinet. The cabinets held caviar, crackers and other nonperishables for her father's clients.

She looked at the caviar, then reached onto the top shelf, where she'd stashed a loaf of twelve-grain bread and a jar of peanut butter. She didn't bother with the bread but got a spoon out of the drawer and carried the jar, spoon and a bottle of Vichy water back to her workstation.

She sat down and pulled up a straight-back chair and put the water and peanut butter on the seat. She'd learned the hard way not to take a chance with food or liquid near her computer.

She stared at the screen while she licked peanut butter off the spoon, and selected the best—or maybe not best but most definitive for documentation—photos and dragged them into one folder that could be presented as a slide show. Then she cross-referenced them to the more inclusive folders.

For the next hour or so, she referenced and cross-referenced, culling out the "arty" photos that she'd taken for herself and putting them into their own folders. She did a quick sweep through the folders again. Closed the program. Stretched her back. Groaned out a yawn.

But instead of going to bed like a responsible working adult, she opened the folder with her photos in it. The ones she'd taken without planning, with no particular purpose other than that they'd caught her eye. The ones that called to her.

"And that's more of your nonsense," she told herself and jumped at the sound of her own voice. It sounded awfully like her father's on their last visit.

That thought, more than her fatigue, should have driven her to bed. But instead, like the stubborn young lady—her mother's words—that she was, she logged into her graphics program and began to play.

Slowly an unidentifiable detail took on a life of its own. She selected two versions, color and black-and-white, overlaid the two, slightly offset in alternating layers, so that if you looked one way it was a color photo and focused another it appeared in black and white. Then relayered in Carlyn's sun-drenched face and hair until a nimbus ran through the entire sequence, the sections nearly transparent as they fanned out like a deck of cards.

She leaned back in her desk chair and surveyed her work. The result sent shivers up her arms. Nice. Really nice. Almost spookily nice. And totally useless. Still, she felt good—a moment of contentment until she noticed the time on her computer screen.

It was past three and she needed to be sharp to navigate the Bruce Stafford-infested waters tomorrow. She hurriedly saved her work and closed the program.

She intended to be there early to set up a projector so she wouldn't have everybody leaning over her to view the stills on her computer screen. She needed to keep her distance. From everyone, even the nice ones.

She certainly needed to keep her distance from Bruce Stafford. Geordie knew her men. And she knew this one was just looking for a reason to get rid of her.

She wasn't about to let that happen.

Chapter 3

•••••••••

BRUCE STAFFORD STOOD at the kitchen window at Gilbert House, nursing a cup of coffee and watching Geordie Holt climb out of her nifty little sports car. She was late. He glanced at his watch. Two minutes, but that's not why he was watching her. He couldn't seem not to.

Meri and Carlyn had been here when he arrived a half hour ago and for a second of relief and disappointment, he'd thought that Geordie had already given up. He could hear them singing some soft rock song as they organized the "business office."

Bruce took another sip of the hot joe, realized he wasn't just watching Geordie Holt, but was staring at her butt. Granted, it was the only part of her he could see. The rest of her had disappeared into the back of the car to retrieve, hopefully, some descent photos.

He was tempted to go out and give her a hand, but he didn't. Just kept looking.

Why was it he could go for weeks at a time without even noticing women, then out of the blue he'd catch himself starting at some inappropriate body part of a complete stranger? Today the inappropriate body part belonged to a beyond totally inappropriate person.

Life was weird. He turned from the window and strode down the hall to Carlyn's office. She was always good for bringing someone back down to earth. Maybe they could talk about the dismal state of the project's finances until he could get his mind off the new photographer.

But when he got there, the two women were standing, heads together, Carlyn holding a cardboard box of ledgers and Meri holding a broom like a microphone, as they gyrated to "Sweet Caroline."

Bruce stood in the doorway until they noticed him. Instead of stopping, they motioned him in. Meri handed him the broom. He wasn't sure if he was supposed to sing into it or start cleaning.

They finished with a choreographed hip-wiggle thing. Carlyn put her box down on an ancient wooden desk and fisted her hands on her hips. "Stop frowning. You should take up karaoke. In fact we just happen to have an opening in our group."

Bruce made a face. "Not in a bucket."

"Really," Meri asked. "What is it about men that none of them can sing?"

"Too macho," said Doug from the doorway. He looked around, then he frowned, too. "Where's—?"

"Unloading her car," Bruce said drily.

Doug shrugged. "Carlyn, would you tell Geordie that on my crew, 'on time' means early?"

Carlyn saluted and headed for the door. Everyone followed her so that they arrived just in time to see the photographer struggling through the back door with an armload of equipment and a portfolio.

Geordie looked up, startled and wary. Carlyn and Meri rushed to take things from her.

She gave them a tentative smile. She looked like shit.

Bruce wanted to give her the benefit of the doubt. Sort of. He'd reserve judgment until he saw what she'd brought them. But if she'd been out partying all night instead of organizing photos, she was history.

"Where do you want to set up?" Meri asked. "Stupid question. You've barely seen the place. What about in the annex, at least it's fairly empty and has electricity."

"Sure."

God, take some initiative, thought Bruce.

Meri and Carlyn started down the hall and Geordie followed them.

"Might as well see what's she's got," Bruce mumbled under his breath.

Doug grabbed his sleeve. "Hold up a sec. Let them get set up."

Bruce turned to face his friend and colleague, already feeling defensive.

"What's up? Are you really not okay with the new photographer? I can kill her if you want, but that will mean Meri will have to do double duty. And she's going to be doing that already until I can come up with some decent interns."

Bruce shook his head.

"It's something else? Want to share?"

"It's me." Bruce shot his fingers through his hair, immediately felt stupid for such a dramatic gesture. "I'm broke, I have way too many clients demanding work, not all of them paying on time, and I should be doing the paying work for them instead of what I want to do here."

"You'll get paid . . . something. But I understand if . . ." Doug shrugged, giving him an out, maybe even expecting Bruce to bail. And he wasn't going to do that, not unless he had to.

Doug was an independent like him. They knew going into it they would always have shoestring budgets at best, and might have to work gratis in between grants.

"I'm in it for the long haul," Bruce said. "I knew what I was getting into when I went solo. I just didn't expect to be so busy."

"Better than the alternative," Doug said.

Bruce cringed. Here he was complaining about being broke, when Doug not only didn't have enough work, couldn't take work that he was qualified for because of his injury and had a family who depended on him.

"Look, do what you need to do but don't get bitter. Nothing is worth that." Doug wasn't bitter, at least not that he showed. He'd recovered and gone about finding a place in restoration work that was satisfying and where he could make a contribution.

"I'm not going to bail." Bruce tried for a grin. "I may have to sleep on your couch."

"Deal. My wife always liked you."

Both of them laughed. It was forced. But it was there and Bruce felt marginally better until they reached the annex. The room was a rectangle, a late addition, probably used for storage or as an additional dining room. It would eventually be pulled down, but for now it was fine for extraneous equipment and occasional meetings.

Meri and Carlyn were moving boxes away from one wall while Geordie set up an expensive-looking projector and connected it to her laptop.

The girl had money from somewhere. Maybe they could make good use of it before she lost interest and moved on.

GEORDIE LOOKED UP when Doug and Bruce entered the room, trying to looked assured but not managing to stop the jaw-cracking yawn that greeted them.

"Must have been some party," Bruce said.

Geordie held back the next yawn. The ass thought she'd been partying all night? That was so typical. She'd been up most of the night working on her presentation. She wasn't even sure what they wanted. A slide show, wide shots then close-ups, or a whole series of wide shots, then another file of close-ups.

And she'd purposely dressed in her worst pair of jeans. There was nothing much she could do about her hair, but she'd kept the makeup light, left off her concealer so the dark under her eyes would let them know she'd spent most of the night working—and they thought she had been partying instead of working.

She turned her back on the architect and booted up her laptop. Spent a minute or two making adjustments and getting her temper under control.

"I thought you might want to see larger shots than you can see on the computer screen, then if you want hard copies, I can print them out."

"That's fine," Doug said and moved to stand off her right shoulder.

Bruce stood over her left.

This is just what she had hoped to avoid, colleagues breathing down her neck while she tried to navigate unfamiliar territory.

Carlyn and Meri filled in until they were standing in a little clump at the table.

Geordie sighed. "Just tell me if you want a hard copy or a different angle and I'll tag the photo."

She clicked on the front facade.

Bruce sighed into her ear. She shifted closer to Doug.

She'd planned a little commentary for the presentation, but the architect was impatient. She moved to the next photo. A close-up of the steps. Then the broken eave ornamentation. The photos continued around the house.

"Hold it."

Geordie's finger froze above the trackpad. What was wrong now?

But Bruce merely leaned over to enlarge a detail and stayed there, talking to Doug over her head. He leaned across her to move the cursor over another detail, brushing against her shoulder as he did. Geordie had to resist the urge to move back.

What was this sense of entitlement, that he just took over her computer like he owned it?

"Hey guys, yoo-hoo," Carlyn called. "Some of us have work to do today. Could you curb your enthusiasm for a minute so we can get through the slides? Geordie will enter them in the database and you can play all you want."

The two men moved away. How did Carlyn do that?

"Go on, Geordie." Carlyn smiled at her, girl to girl, and Geordie felt marginally better.

She showed another photo.

"Hold it. Isn't this another shot of the front steps?"

"Yes."

"It's out of order. You should have kept this photo with number . . . Are these photos numbered?"

Geordie didn't answer. They were in order, or so she'd thought.

"They are time coded on my camera."

"Well, they have to be time coded in the data that accompanies each photo. Which includes sector number, and detailed notes."

Sector number? No one had told her about sector numbers. Had they even been in the house long enough to have drawn up sector numbers?

"You didn't do any of this, did you?"

She could lie but what good would it do? She must have missed that chapter when she was cramming for the job. Of course it made sense and if she'd been thinking clearly and known what she was doing, she would have realized it. But from the minute she shook hands with Doug, she'd been totally busy trying not to drown.

Her ears began to ring, and she tried furiously to think of something calming so her skin wouldn't flush and give her away.

"What's the point of wasting time and money taking shots if we don't know what the hell we're looking at?"

"My fault," Carlyn said calmly. "I was so busy I forgot to rustle up the forms we use. I'll get them when we finish and enter the data then."

Bruce scowled at her. Carlyn wasn't fooling him or anybody else. But why was she covering for her? Why?

"But like I said, some of us have work to do. Things like applying for a few more grants so Geordie will have a reason to take photos." She gave Doug what Geordie guessed must be her version of an evil eye, but it held more humor than demand.

"Right. Go on, Geordie." Doug turned back to the screen.

Geordie went through photo after photo, naming the area and explaining the detail. There was nothing wrong with her memory. She recognized most of them and hedged the others. She might have to go over the house to refresh her memory, but by God, she'd have them entered correctly before tomorrow.

She opened another file and ran through the stills of each room. She tagged the photos to be detailed and moved them into a separate file. The room had become totally quiet. So quiet that Geordie could here the cars on the street. A motorcycle rumbling at the stop sign. The radio from a road crew on the next block.

"Next."

The words almost in her ear startled her. She'd let her mind wander again. She had high powers of concentration if she was interested in something.

She'd always been that way. Her mother had even had her tested for ADD, but she passed with flying colors.

They said it was a discipline problem. She should try harder. But she'd seen something outside the window by then and hadn't heard what they said.

She switched to the foyer file. The octagonal walls, the front door, transom window. A close-up of several portions of the glass design. As much of the ceiling as she could get from the floor. Geordie stifled another yawn. She needed another cup of coffee. Zoomed in where the paint was thin and revealed a play of dark and light. A pattern beneath the paint. That would be interesting.

The corner molding. The window sill. The shaft of light pricking the wood and fanning into a dozen sections and the arc of light—

"What the hell is that?"

"Sorry." Geordie moved quickly to the next photo. She must have been tired to get things mixed up like that. And even more tired by the time she clicked through this morning before breakfast to make sure she'd gotten all she needed.

She sat up, refocused. No more slips like that. *Mind on your work, mind on your work, mind on your work.*

"Wait a minute." Meri leaned over the computer. "That was amazing. Can we see it?"

"Maybe you girls could look at it later?" Bruce said. "Doug and I need to get to work."

What did he think the rest of them were doing? Oh, how she was tempted just to tell him off. And he would fire her, which would put her right back where she didn't want to be, headed for Daddy's corporate office.

Carlyn rolled her eyes. Meri pressed her lips together. They were more amused than upset. Maybe Geordie was just oversensitive.

She sped through the rest of the slides, tagging and ditching and counting to ten, twenty, a hundred. Then it was finished. She waited for the architect to pass judgment.

But all Bruce said was, "Okay. Put the tagged ones in one file and send it to the database along with all the rest. With all the data filled in."

He walked out of the room.

"Good work," Doug said and patted her shoulder, which was almost as bad as being barked at.

As soon as they left, Meri sat down. "You'll have to forgive the boys, they get into the zone and forget their manners. You got some great photos."

Geordie just looked at her.

"So now can we see the photo you were so quick to hide? I may be going crazy but I swear I saw Carlyn's face in that photo."

"No way," Carlyn said, moving closer.

Geordie pulled a face. "It just got in there by mistake. It was late when I decided on the final presentation"—*for all the good it did me*—"and it just slipped past me."

"And we're glad it did." Meri pulled up a chair. "Show."

Geordie scrolled through the photos until she got to the

"Wood" photo. She took a breath and opened it. It appeared on the wall before them.

"Wow," Meri said.

"What is it?" Carlyn asked.

"Me playing," Geordie said. "There was this shaft of light hitting the windowsill." She moved the cursor to a separate image. "That's the original. It looked like it pierced the wood, like it would shatter it, but not in pieces like glass but in slices revealing the form in black-and-white as well as the manifestation in color. But right after that, I caught the sun glowing on Carlyn's hair, not shattering it but glowing and—" She stopped abruptly.

Carlyn looked puzzled. "That's me?"

Meri smiled. "I can see where your interest lies."

"No, I—"

"No need to explain, but why are you here doing documentation photos, when you could be showing your work in a gallery? Or do you do both?"

Geordie shook her head. She couldn't speak. Meri was being nice, even enthusiastic, but her tone of voice said that Geordie had blown this job.

She'd tried so hard and she'd only lasted one day.

Chapter 4

. . . .

"You have to admit she's not bad," Doug said pouring coffee and handing a mug to Bruce.

"She can take a decent picture, but there was a lot of garbage in there. She doesn't have a clue about what her job is. She didn't even have the sense to ask what documentation form we use."

"So she's green. It was her first day. She hadn't even been walked through the site and was working cold."

"That's beside the point."

"Is it? Then tell her what you want and how you want it and—"

Bruce burst out laughing. "You sound like one of Meri and Carlyn's karaoke songs." Bruce wiggled in a gross parody of the two women singing that morning in the office.

"You're hired."

Bruce spun around, nearly spilling his coffee.

The three women were standing in the doorway of the kitchen.

Meri and Carlyn were grinning. Geordie looked like she'd just eaten glass.

Okay, he was an idiot. And he'd just been riding Geordie for being unprofessional. Some example he was setting.

Carlyn came in and poured herself a cup of coffee. Held up the pot to the other two. Both declined. "The office is halfway organized, so I'm returning Meri and Geordie to you for assignment."

Doug glanced at his watch. "I have a crew coming in to clean at ten. They should be fairly thorough, half interns and half pros. But Meri, if you will keep an eye on them and make sure they don't cart anything valuable away or break anything..."

He turned to Geordie. "You can take a couple of shots of the crew just for the record, then explore the first floor if you want or you can take the rest of the day off."

Geordie shot Bruce a look that confused him. She was pissed. At him? What did he do?

She heaved a sigh, not really a sigh, more like taking a deep breath.

"I'll stick around, if that's okay. There are plenty of things to be documented *in situ*, as is, before they're restored to their former glory." She narrowed her eyes at Bruce. "For the record."

"What the—? Fine." Just when he was about to think she was okay, she copped an attitude. Who the hell did she think she was? He stopped as the answer hit him. That was what pushed his buttons. Not the fancy car, the expensive camera equipment, not even the designer jeans.

It was because she was some dilettante rich kid out on a lark who would leave as soon as she lost interest. She didn't need this job. Hell, she could pay for a good chunk of the restoration for what she probably paid for that car. He could probably survive for a whole year on the same amount. Hell, she'd laugh if he invited her to dinner, she probably ate at five-star restaurants.

He reached for his notebook. He'd spent hours last night calculating specs and working out scheduling for demolition and reconstruction, while Miss Fancy Pants was out getting wasted and probably having hot sex all night.

He logged in, then stood glaring at the women until they left the room.

Doug shook his head and leaned over the fact sheet.

"I know," Bruce said. "I'm just a little stressed these days. Sorry."

"Look if you don't have the time, I understand. I've been there. I had to turn down lots of work when I started out, because I had to work paying construction jobs. Made me crazy."

"But you stuck it out."

Doug straightened up. "Having second thoughts?"

"No. And I could make it fine if some of my clients would actually pay me. But it seems the richer they are the slower they are in paying."

"Which is probably why they're rich."

"Probably."

"Look, if you need to spend some time on your other work, do it. We've got enough work to keep us busy. I've got a call in to a couple of carpenters. They can handle the changes. Catch up with your other work. We'll still be here." He chuckled. "Actually, we haven't paid you either."

"You're different. I want to do this and nobody else is being paid yet, except that party girl, and if you ask me she doesn't need the money."

"Maybe not, but she takes a damn good photograph."

"Jeez." Carlyn said as they walked tandem back to the office. "Feeling a little tense, are we?"

"I know." Meri pantomimed strangling herself. "I probably should have stayed to see the numbers, but I was afraid he was going to blow."

"Is he always this nasty?" Geordie asked. "Or . . . or is it just me that sets him off?"

"You?" Carlyn stopped and threw her arm around Geordie's shoulder.

It took her by surprise and she nearly flinched away.

"Why do you think it's you?"

Geordie shrugged but didn't answer.

When they reached Carlyn's office, Meri closed the door. "I don't know Bruce very well. I've never worked on a project with him. But Doug doesn't allow histrionics on a project, does he Carlyn?"

"Only his own. Fortunately the worst he gets is teddy-bear-on-a-tear. I don't know about Bruce, but I bet you money, Doug's in the kitchen telling him to lighten up."

Geordie took a breath. Her throat tightened. "Maybe I should just . . ."

"Don't quit," they said simultaneously.

It made Geordie smile and at this point she didn't think she had a smile left.

"At least not until after lunch," Carlyn said. "We'll go out. Meri can't do anything until the cleaners are gone except help them haul garbage. Totally a waste of her talent. And I can't face the non-state of our non-finances on an empty stomach."

"Is it really that bad?"

"Always. And total mayhem at the start. But somehow we keep muddling through. Meri, remember the first day on the Wilkinses' Farm?"

"Do I have to? The stone house had survived for almost two hundred years up until it was declared a historic home and okayed for restoration. We walked into a foot of water. A pipe had burst. Fortunately it happened only that morning. You've never seen people move so fast to pump out the water before it stained the fieldstone."

"You've all worked together a long time?"

"Yeah," Meri said. "I weaseled my way into an internship with Doug while I was in college, before I really knew what I was doing."

Geordie's stomach bottomed out. Was Meri giving her a subtle hint?

Carlyn thumped her chest. "I fortunately knew what I was doing from the get-go."

"Finance major," Meri said. "I got her hooked on architecture and the rest is history."

"That's really neat. I mean that you're friends and colleagues and everything."

The two women exchanged smiles, a kind of camaraderie Geordie couldn't remember having.

"Yeah it is," Carlyn said.

"And karaoke partners," Meri added. "Hey, it's hard being the new kid. You'll find your way. By the way, can you sing?"

BRUCE LEFT THE plans with Doug and drove to Middletown to check on the progress of the Lovells' bathroom renovation, stopping only long enough to drive through a fast-food place and down a hamburger while he drove.

The fixtures had been put in, the plumbers had come and gone. He spent the afternoon measuring and laying backsplash tile, while one tiler came in to do the cuts.

It was dark by the time he climbed back into his old Kia and headed for home. Man and car both needed a bath, and the Kia needed new brakes. Like that was going to happen. He might be biking it before the winter set in. Or maybe the Lowells would give him a big tip.

He'd meant to check on a kitchen/great room demolition, but he was just too tired. But he did swing by to see if Doug was still on-site.

Doug's car was gone, but Carlyn's was in the parking lot, along with Meri's bike and Geordie's little sports car. The Dumpster had been delivered and was already piled high with junk. He probably should have stayed to help oversee the clean out, but Meri was more than capable. He was just turning into a control freak and that was not a good thing.

He parked at the back door and took a few deep breaths before going inside. The hall was dark but he could hear laughter coming from down the hall.

It was coming from the annex. What could the girls be doing in there at this hour?

He groped his way toward the sound and poked his head in the open door. The room was only partially lit, enough to show a pizza box and a six-pack of soda. The three of them were sitting at the table behind Geordie's laptop.

Were they helping her to organize her slides? Honestly, if she couldn't do the most basic work by herself, she really needed to be off the project.

She saw him first. Froze like a deer in headlights then jabbed at the projector. The room suddenly went dark. Leaving the women barely silhouetted against the little light from the hall.

Carlyn stood and a second later the overhead light came on.

No one gave him any kind of explanation. Just looked.

"Is Doug still around?" he asked, knowing it was a stupid question, because Doug's car was gone.

"He left about an hour ago, " Meri said. "We've just been looking at—" She broke off. "Can I do anything for you?"

"No." They were acting awfully suspicious. "Did you finish documenting your photos?"

Geordie didn't answer. Damn her, he wasn't an ogre. "Well?"

Carlyn struck one of her poses. "Signed."

Meri mimicked the same pose. "Sealed."

He waited, but Geordie didn't join in. She just gave him a look, then shoved a thick manila envelope across the table.

Bruce barely caught it before it hit the ground.

"Hard copy and I e-mailed you the file."

He studied the three women. He'd bet money that's why they were all three still here. They had helped her. Anger welled up inside him. He tamped it down. What did it matter to him if they wanted to help her? She'd just better start carrying her weight, and soon.

He took the folder, glanced inside. It was thorough, to judge by the first few pages. "Just lock up when you're done." God, he sounded like a condescending jackass. "I mean . . ."

"We know what you mean, and we'll be sure to check everything before we leave." Meri smiled at him. "Especially our naughty-and-nice list." She was joking but she was letting him know he had stepped over the line. "Twice."

Brue nodded. He deserved that. He really needed to get a grip. Maybe he should make a doctor's appointment.

He didn't need tranquilizers, he needed more time, more money . . . he needed to lighten up and give his business plan more time or go back to working in a firm and quit being an ass to his colleagues because he was screwing up.

He hid a yawn behind his fist; his eyes were gritty from tile dust and lack of sleep.

"Must have been some party." Geordie smiled back at him, not friendly but a combination of sarcasm, anger, and challenge.

He didn't have the energy or the patience to play that game. "Good night." He retreated into the hallway.

"WHEW," CARLYN SAID. "That boy needs some smacking." She grinned. "And I wouldn't mind doing it, except he's just too damn intense for me."

"And I've got a boyfriend," Meri said. "Soon to be fiancé. Besides it doesn't really work to get involved with your co-workers."

They both looked at Geordie.

Geordie shook her head, "You don't have to warn me. He's good-looking, but I'm with Carlyn, way too uptight. Plus he doesn't like me."

"Huh," Carlyn said. "Maybe he just needs some love."

Meri pushed her chair back. "I don't know about Bruce, but I know I do. Can you guys close up? I've got to go home and change so I can do-wah-diddy all night."

Carlyn sighed. "I guess I'll go home and wash my hair."

Meri laughed. "Don't let her fool you. She's got a stable of . . ."

"Don't say it. Commitment-phobic hunks."

"I was just going to say hunks. But yeah, she really knows how to pick them."

Carlyn rolled her eyes and began cleaning up the pizza leftovers.

Meri dumped their paper plates in a garbage bag. "So I'll be busy tomorrow , but Sunday is supposed to be nice. Peter's working on a brief, and I'm going out to see Gran. Might be our last beach day. Want to come?"

"I'm in," Carlyn said.

"How about you, Geordie? If you're free, you're welcome to come. My grandmother lives across the bridge on a farm near Little Compton. It's right on the ocean. Private beach. Good food. And she loves company."

It sounded great but were they just being polite? Should she stay home and work? Brood? Worry?

"You can ride out with me," Carlyn said. "You could get some great shots of the farm and the bay."

"Well ... okay ... thanks."

They carried the trash and recycling back to the kitchen. Meri left but Carlyn and Geordie doubled-checked windows and doors, and turned off all the lights before closing up the house for the weekend.

"When things start moving we'll be working all the time, even on Sundays whenever Doug's wife will let him. Sometimes without him. But you won't need to be on-site all the time. You'll have time for your other work."

Alarmed, Geordie blurted. "I don't have other work."

"I mean your other photos. You know they're very good. They should be in a gallery. Meri thinks so, too, and she knows her stuff."

Geordie gave her a weak smile. That's how this whole thing started, when she'd announced that she was going to be a professional art photographer. It's what she really wanted to do. It was obvious after tonight and the way Meri and Carlyn had reacted to her portfolio that that was where her talent lay.

She'd known it for a while. Even while trying to fit it into another job, which would bring her "security" and teach her "responsibility." Like her sisters. Alicia and Kendra were professionals—marketing and pediatrics—and married—podiatrist and lawyer.

Geordie thought project photographer might satisfy her father. It sounded pretty good, but basically it was a job with no future. No ladder to the corner office—not even a husband.

But Meri and Carlyn, Doug, and even Bruce Stafford were passionate about their work. Lived for it. Gave up other more lucrative careers for it.

Geordie wanted to have that fire and the only times she felt it were when she was photographing . . . in the zone, as it were . . . or in the darkroom or at the computer working with her photos.

But how could she convince her dad?

They said Bruce was stressed. Well, she knew the feeling.

Ordinarily when life got to be too much, she'd go out to a party or a bar, have a few drinks, dance, maybe pick up some decent guy for a one nighter. She couldn't remember the last time she'd had a steady lover. And "boyfriend?" It was a quaint and yet oddly tempting idea. Unfortunately, she'd never met anyone who kept her interest for more than a few days.

She wondered if Bruce had a steady relationship with someone.

"Don't even think it." She liked the way he looked, kind of got off on his intensity when it wasn't directed toward her. But she knew better than to pursue it. She knew exactly where that would lead. Not to love, but straight out the door with a pink slip.

Chapter 5

....

EARLY SUNDAY MORNING, Geordie slung a stuffed beach bag and her waterproof camera bag across her chest and set off to meet Carlyn. The day was already sunny and warm and she was looking forward to a day at the beach.

She was also a little nervous. She liked Carlyn and Meri, but she knew very little about them. And they knew practically nothing about her, which is the way she wanted it.

She'd insisted on walking over to Carlyn's apartment because she didn't want them to see where she lived. Have it draw a line between them. Have to explain that it wasn't really hers. All the things you found out about people as you got to know them.

She wanted to be taken seriously, not be thought of as the rich, aimless person she was. Besides she was really enjoying the work.

And not just photographing the site. She'd helped Carlyn

rearrange the furniture in her office. Then Meri asked her to help her roll out plastic to cover some wood inlay. Everyone on the team pitched in where and when they were needed. And before Geordie realized it, she'd joined in the spirit of the others. Strangely enough she began to feel excitement, found herself taking ownership in the project herself.

Only Bruce blamed Geordie for not having experience. Doug had complimented her work. Meri and Carlyn didn't judge her, but helped bring her up to speed.

The more Geordie learned about Doug's team, the more her mind started going places she'd promised herself not to go. Here were people who lived from paycheck to paycheck, saving what money they could for when there were no checks. Who were content hanging out at the neighborhood karaoke bar, or eating lunch on the steps of an old house.

And they loved their work.

Geordie loved the way they got excited over simple things. Like Meri, rapt as she stared up at that god-awful painted ceiling. Doug marking up the floor plans with a flourish of an artist. Even Bruce, the ogre, hunched over the front steps, speculating what might be underneath decades of paint and plaster and grime.

She understood what they were seeing. Felt their anticipation, the possibilities. Wasn't it the same with her when she saw something that was more than what it appeared? Something that her eye could capture and transform . . .

Geordie arrived at Carlyn's much too soon. She was looking forward to the day but also was a little nervous. She shifted her bags and walked up the steps of an old house with four mailboxes hanging on the front wall. It was funky and lived-in. As she opened the door, a man holding a child in one arm and a tricycle in the other, called out, "Hold the door."

Geordie did and stayed to watch as the girl climbed on and pedaled down the sidewalk, her father walking briskly behind her.

Carlyn lived on the first floor. She answered the door wrapped in a towel. "Come on in. I'm almost ready. Just running a tad late."

Geordie walked into the smallest combination living room and kitchen she'd seen since her summer abroad in Ibiza, where she photographed Greek ruins and dark native children playing in the streets.

She could see through to a small bedroom that was filled with morning light and half-packed cardboard boxes.

"Are you moving?"

"No, can't afford to. My roommate is going to grad school in California. I'll have to start looking for another one." She shuddered dramatically. "It's so hard to find someone you can put up with and vice versa."

Geordie nodded. She couldn't imagine being confined to such a small space.

"I'm almost ready. Just have a seat."

Geordie sat on a vintage couch that sagged in the middle and was threadbare on the arms.

"Overslept." Carlyn called from the second bedroom. She came out a minute later dressed in yellow jeans and an orange striped tee under a black hoodie. She rummaged through her oversized purse, tossing out a book, makeup, papers, and a calculator onto the tiny kitchen counter. Finally, she extracted a wallet and a pair of sunglasses and stuffed them into an even larger tote.

Geordie stood. "Are you sure it's okay with Meri's grandmother if I show up?"

"I'm sure. The more the merrier. Gran loves company and she's a great cook."

Geordie swallowed. She hoped she wouldn't feel awkward and totally out of place.

"Come on. Sun's out. Let's get hopping; there won't be many more days like this."

Carlyn's car was parked at the curb half a block away. They threw their stuff in the back seat and jumped in.

It was the end of September, and they were having a bit of an Indian summer. And a brief respite from tourists, a few days between the end of one tourist season and before the fall leaves drew a whole new set of people

Traffic, always heavy on weekends, was moving steadily but slowly and a few minutes later they were turning onto Memorial Boulevard heading east toward the bridge that would lead them to the peninsula and farmland.

Geordie leaned back against the seat, closed her eyes and breathed in the fresh air. There was something about the air around the ocean, the sun over water, something she'd like to capture with her camera, the sight, the taste, the smell, the feel. All through the lens. She knew she could do it. That was her passion. It just didn't pay the rent.

And would never satisfy her parents.

"What?"

Geordie opened her eyes and looked over at Carlyn. "What about what?"

"News alert. Humongous sigh from the passenger seat. Or was that a snore?"

Geordie laughed. "I guess it was a sigh."

"Good or bad sigh? Or a none-of-my-business sigh?"

"Oh, good. I guess. Just taking in the freedom."

"Huh. Riding in an old clunker make you feel free?"

Geordie shifted to face Carlyn. "It does today. Anyway it's a classy old clunker."

Carlyn grinned at her. "I guess you had a rough week. You'll get your chops down soon. Don't know why Bruce Stafford is being such a jerk to you. Doug says he's under a lot of pressure."

Geordie snorted. "From what?" She bet he didn't have a family that totally disapproved of his choice of professions. There was nothing wrong with being an architect. *There was nothing wrong with being a photographer either.*

"Money, I think. If you haven't noticed, none of us will retire with a pension. Hell, none of us will ever be able to retire, period."

"Do you ever think about doing something else? I mean you could get a job in finance and make a lot more."

"Meri would kill me if I tried to leave." Carlyn grinned. "She'd probably even kick me out of our karaoke group."

"You stay just for her?"

"God, no. I love it. It's a pain in my butt trying to raise enough money, but it's addictive. You should see our other houses. Doug used to be a great conservator, engineer, painter, carpenter. Amazing.

"What happened to him?"

"Fell through a second-story floor, broke his leg and hip in several places. He's pinned together. Will never go up another ladder. At least not to work. So he struck out on his own. Finds the buildings. Convinces someone to bankroll him enough to get started, then I go in and try to drum up support while Meri and everyone else works like nutcases to make silk purses out of some really butt-ugly sow's ears. It's the best job in the world."

"I guess you like it a little."

"Yep."

Geordie saw the sign for the bridge across the Sakonnet River. She closed her eyes. Not relaxed this time, but clearing her head of all thoughts, breathing deeply until they were across.

They turned south and drove along a county road, passed through the little town of Tiverton and into farm country. Some fields were still green, some were just turning golden or brown. Some were mown, and some were still ripening, their stalks crowded and swaying as one in the ocean breeze. The air was tangy with salt and Geordie was sure she could hear the rush of the waves on the shore.

It wasn't long before they turned down a long drive that led between grassy dunes toward two houses. The nearest one was several stories tall, dark shingled, with alcoves and heavy eaves, a Gothic menace that even the sunlight couldn't brighten.

She was relieved when Carlyn drove past it and pulled into the next drive. She stopped in front of a stone-and-clapboard farmhouse. Meri's car was already parked at the far side.

"Welcome to Calder Farm," Carlyn said. "Isn't it fabulous?"

"It is."

An older woman came to the door and waved as they got out of the car.

"Hey Gran." Carlyn leaned forward to give the woman a kiss. "This is Geordie. She just came to work with the team. Geordie this is Therese Calder, Meri's grandmother. We all call her Gran."

Geordie stuck out her hand.

"Welcome Geordie," Therese said, shaking her hand. Then held it long enough to give it a pat. She was a tall woman, not old, not young, or maybe both. Geordie could practically see the stories written in the fine lines created by her smile. She itched to get out her camera.

"Thank you for having me, Mrs. Calder."

"You're very welcome. And you can certainly call me Gran. I don't know if I'd answer to my own name around Meri's friends." She released Geordie's hand. "Make yourself at home."

"Where's Meri?" Carlyn asked as they walked into a cozy, sweet-smelling kitchen.

"She took an apple pie over the way, to Alden. Don't worry, I made two. She'll be coming back; I'm sure she heard your car. Take your things upstairs to the guest bedroom to change if you're planning to swim."

"You know we are. This might be the last swim of the

season." Carlyn planted another kiss on Therese Calder's cheek; Geordie smiled at her and followed Carlyn up the stairs.

Meri was waiting for them in the kitchen when they came down dressed for the beach, and in Geordie's case, laden with her camera bag. She planned to get some good shots today.

She'd spent way too many years wasting time in the sun and surf with drinks and men without taking a single photo.

Mrs. Calder handed Meri a cooler of food and a thermos of iced tea and watched from the door as they crossed the dunes.

Geordie glanced back, and Mrs. Calder waved. Geordie could feel the love between Meri and her grandmother, and Therese Calder—Gran—managed to spread it to Carlyn and Geordie. It was pretty cool.

Meri led the way down an eroded sand path between tall grasses and sea roses. It took some concentration not to slide all the way to the water, and Geordie was a little winded when they finally arrived on a small half moon sheltered on one side by the dunes and on the ocean side by the rocks of a breakwater that curved from the headland. The sun was warm and the waves were tame.

They stood on a patch of soft white sand.

To their left the beach gradually became coarser until it turned into pebbles that became darker and a bit foreboding. Behind it, the roof of the Gothic mansion rose above the dunes, evocative and a little scary. To the right a clump of sea roses led to a point where the land joined the breakwater.

"This is an amazing place," Geordie said. "Is it all your family's, Meri?"

"Yeah," Meri said and flicked her eyes toward the menacing Gothic house. "Well, we share it with Alden, but he's like family."

As they spread out their towels, Geordie wondered if they would catch a glimpse of the eccentric neighbor before they left. She pulled off her top and jeans and lay back. There was hardly any breeze on the sheltered beach and the sun beat down, warming her, as she watched the clouds drift overhead.

She hadn't been aware of how really tense she'd been until she felt herself melt into the contours of the sand, her muscles grow heavy and her eyelids began to droop. It had been a stressful week.

Between working late to satisfy the ogre architect and lying awake worried about her future, she was bone tired. And now that she finally had the chance to relax, the adrenalin that had kept her going fled and she was left with a sense of peace.

It wouldn't last. Nothing ever did, but for now . . .

Meri and Carolyn lay beside her, eyes closed, both in their own worlds, or maybe asleep.

One woman, dark haired with fair skin, slightly ethereal, the other colorful and robust—the odd couple and great friends. Carlyn's energy calm as she sprawled face up in the sun, stripped down to a string bikini. Meri's energy creating an aura around her even as she lay on an old beach blanket, her bikini covered with a zipped hoodie and her legs bare to the sun.

Geordie automatically reached for her camera. Knew if she started whirring away, the mood would be destroyed.

"I'm going to take some shots of the dunes," she said.

Carlyn languidly raised a hand. Meri opened her eyes and turned her head enough to see her. "Have fun."

"I will." Geordie headed for the dunes. They formed a wall behind the beach and were covered with green shrubs and tall grasses so green and vibrant that it took her breath away. The sun drifted behind one of the white puffy clouds overhead, sweeping a change of color over the grasses. And returning to full color a moment later.

Soon she was settled into the *whirr, whirr* of photographing, and the rest of the world disappeared. She zeroed in on the colors and textures of the dunes. Took close-ups of animal tracks until they turned into pure design. Turned back to capture some candid shots of Meri and Carlyn.

She lay down on the sand propped on one elbow, so that she could aim the camera through a curtain of sticky sea grass at the two women on the beach. The grass created a kind of filter, blurring the figures until they were mere hints of color. Then she sat up and zoomed in just as Carlyn stood up and walked out to the surf. Geordie followed her with the lens.

Carlyn turned back, shielding her eyes with her hand. She saw Geordie and waved. "Come have lunch."

The mood was broken. Geordie had no idea how long she'd been there taking shots and she felt a bit like a voyeur. She hadn't even asked if it was okay to photograph them. But wasn't that the point? To capture the feel without the subject being aware of the camera?

She was stiff. And embarrassed. How rude could she be, to be invited for the day at the beach and then use the friends who invited her as subjects? But Carlyn merely grinned back at her and struck a pose. She got off one more shot and staggered to her feet.

"Get anything good?" Carlyn asked as she plopped down beside her.

"I think so," Geordie said. Actually she'd taken some terrific shots of both land and friends.

Meri sat up, pulled back her hood and shook out her hair before reaching for the cooler. "We'd better eat this before it gets any later," she said as she passed out sandwiches and crudité.

"I hope you guys are planning to stay for dinner, because Gran is making her special rosemary chicken and there's homemade apple pie. I already had a piece at Alden's and it's delish."

"He lives in that big house over there?" Geordie looked back at the peaked roofs of the dark house. Except for a sun-porch that overlooked the ocean, it was just as dark as it had been in her first impression. "It's kind of sinister-looking."

Meri laughed. "It isn't. It's just that Alden lives there alone and works there when he isn't traveling. He doesn't really have the time to keep things fixed up. Plus he's kind of a recluse."

"Kind of . . . ?" Carlyn laughed. "I've never even seen him."

"Because you never get out here. He's perfectly fine. Our families have been neighbors for generations. They were actually working farms at one time. He's been a part of the family for as long as I can remember. I'm glad he's here to look out for Gran." Meri smiled and Geordie tried to think back to her childhood and realized she had no idea who lived in any of the huge houses in the neighborhood where she grew up.

Poor little rich girl, she thought and laughed at herself. She had nothing to complain about.

After the lunch and the trash was packed away, Meri stood and shook the sand from her clothes. "I'm going out to the breakers. You can see the whole ocean from there. It's one of my favorite places. Anyone want to come ?"

Carlyn jumped up, grabbed her sweatshirt, and shoved her feet into sneakers. "You should come, Geordie. It's a spectacular view. But put on shoes, some of the rocks are sharp."

Geordie looked out at the black rocks. It looked kind of dangerous, but not all that high. She shrugged back into her sweatshirt, put on her shoes, and fixed the camera strap over her shoulder.

"When the tide comes in you have to wade back to land," Meri said as they walked single file across the sand. "And in a storm, well, you better get the hell to land, because you'll be stuck out there for the duration."

Geordie looked at the sky. It was brilliant blue. But she could imagine.

They followed a narrow pathway through the beach grasses until they reached the rocks, which suddenly loomed taller than their heads. They were a lot larger than they had looked from the beach, Geordie realized. And a lot higher. She felt a familiar tightening of her throat.

Meri began to climb. Carlyn followed her, but Geordie

hung back while she imagined a calm, safe place. She pushed her camera behind her as she groped for handholds on the jagged rocks. Focusing on the rough surface of the rocks ahead, she pushed one foot until it found a flat place on the boulder.

The other two were farther ahead of her now and Geordie risked a look up to see how much farther she had to go.

Carlyn was a shadow against the sun, but Meri had climbed to the crest of the jetty and stood feet planted between two boulders, her hair and clothes whipping in a blustery ocean wind.

Geordie hesitated, suddenly longing to be back on the sheltered beach. But when she turned to see how far she had come, the world went out of focus. Her heart began beating frantically, her throat tightened until she couldn't draw breath.

Dizziness overcame her and she threw herself backward against the hard rock and squeezed her eyes shut. *Calm down. Turn around, and climb down.*

"Hey, are you coming? Are you stuck?"

She heard Carlyn call her, but her voice seemed far away.

"Are you okay?" Meri's voice, concerned.

Geordie could only wave them off. Why had she looked back? She'd been fine until then. She grabbed her camera with both hands, saw them shaking, and slid down the rough edge of rock until she was sitting with her back pressed against the hard surface. Steadied the camera and looked through the lens until the dizziness and panic began to subside.

She fought back tears of fear and frustration. *It's not even that high, you dummy.* All she needed to do was stand up, follow Carlyn and Meri to the top like anybody else on earth would do. But all she could do was squat there, clutching her camera and staring through the lens at the black hard rock at her feet.

By the time they reached her, she had almost recovered. "Did I miss it? Sorry, I got wrapped up in taking some shots."

"I'll say. Get anything good?" Carlyn asked.

She risked a glance at Meri. Meri just smiled back at her.

"Yeah, I think so. Can't help myself." She waited for Carlyn and Meri to pass her, jumping from boulder to boulder, then she slid the rest of the way down, clutching her camera and grabbing at handholds, until her feet found soft sand again.

Chapter 6

· · · · · · · · ·

GEORDIE WAS RIDING on a high when she got to work the next morning. Gran Calder had made her feel so welcome that she forgot her panic on the rocks. The rest of the day had been wonderful. Dinner was simple and delicious, served at the old kitchen table with no fanfare, but with plenty of love. They'd all gone home with extra pieces of pie, which Geordie had eaten for breakfast.

There were already several trucks in the back parking lot of Gilbert House, so Geordie pulled to the far side and parked under an old tree. She carried her equipment inside and looked into the kitchen, but it was empty. She could hear hammering from down the hall, so she followed the noise to the foyer, where the others were standing in a semicircle around—Gulp.

"Hey," Meri said. "My scaffolding is almost finished."

She sounded like Christmas morning. Geordie felt a

creeping dread that started in the pit of her stomach and radiated out until her fingers tingled.

"Wow," she managed. "I better put my stuff away." She hurried down the hall to the annex and closed the door as soon as she was inside. What was wrong with her? It was a scaffold, for heaven's sake. Not more than two stories high. And she'd prepare herself . . . if she had to.

She took a deep breath, blew it out her mouth. Took another. Besides, there wouldn't be any reason for her to have to go up there. She had a powerful zoom lens. But what if . . .

She began to methodically lay out cameras and lenses that she would need for the day. Set up her laptop so she could transfer as she went, and not have to guess what the hell the pictures were like last week. Nothing like a load of extra work to speed up your learning curve. She was determined to appear calm, cool, and professional no matter what.

She had just picked up her zoom lens, when a shadow appeared in the doorway. She didn't have to look up to know who it was. Her nemesis.

"Good morning," she said, taking the initiative. She smiled brightly at him, even though he couldn't manage to do anything but scowl. If possible he looked more tired than he had on Friday.

She decided to keep her sarcasm to herself.

"I know how you got this job."

That made her look up. "I applied for it just like everyone else."

"But not everyone has a family as influential as yours."

She stared at him. "I—" She'd gotten this job on her

own, the portfolio, the interview, it was all her. She hadn't mentioned her family and God knew Holt was a common-enough name. "Who told you that?"

"That doesn't matter. But you should know you're costing us a lot of money."

"What is it with you? I was hired—for a salary—just like the rest of you."

"Right. Sure you were. Just try not to screw up until I—we—can replace you."

He was gone. Her first instinct was to run after him and tell him he was wrong. Was he just guessing because somehow he had found out who her family was? Or was it true? Had they hired her as a favor to dear old Dad?

She flushed hot, her throat burned and she had to dig her nails into her palms to keep the tears of anger and frustration building in her eyes from overflowing.

"You're an ass, Bruce Stafford," she said to the empty room. She ran her knuckles beneath her eyes, picked up her camera and tripod and went to work.

She'd planned to start as far from Meri's scaffolding as possible, but she ran into Carlyn, who was on her way back to her office.

"Oh, good. Meri needs some shots of her ceiling. Just to bring you up to speed, the medallion is heavy, sagging, and creating cracks in the plaster and Doug wants to have it inspected before she starts on it. She's like a horse at the starting gate. So please go get some identifying shots so she can start work."

Geordie nodded. She probably could get everything from

the ground. If not, she'd just focus on her cameras until she got to the top . . . She swayed on her feet. *Stop it. Stop it.* She can do this. Yesterday had been an aberration.

She'd almost overcome her fear of heights, something she'd had since childhood. "Not necessarily from a trauma," the doctor had said. Some people are just hardwired that way."

She'd had the balance tests, done the shrink thing, and finally had success with behavioral therapy. Until last year, when she'd taken a nosedive, literally and figuratively, down the side of a canyon wall. Granted, it had been a little bitty canyon wall and she'd been properly harnessed. But it still had scared her spitless and undid all the therapy she'd gone through before.

She still hadn't gone back for the refresher course.

She walked into the foyer. There was no sign of the workmen, just Doug and Bruce looking up at Meri, who waved from high above their heads. "This is fabulous."

"Yeah." Geordie breathed and looked up long enough to feel the room begin to spin.

"Oh, good. Carlyn found you." Doug strode toward her.

"Will you please climb up there and take some shots so she'll come back down and do the work I want her to do?"

"I can probably get it from down here. I've got a pretty powerful zoom lens. If Meri just points—" *Shut up. Stop talking. Stay calm.*

Bruce appeared at Doug's shoulder. "Just go up there so she can show you what she wants."

Jeez. Why did he have to be so nasty all the time? It was

such a shame, because he was fit, good-looking, and had a brain. And also had it out for her.

Meri looked down at them. "That's okay. I'll get them later. No need for both of us to be up here."

"That's what she's being paid for." Bruce turned on Geordie. "Anytime today would be good."

Geordie gritted her teeth. Stepped toward the scaffolding. Her heart was thumping so hard in her chest she thought it could break bones.

"Really, it's unnecessary," Meri called.

"Now," Bruce said. His eyes were locked on Geordie.

Geordie stopped. She would take the chance of humiliating herself in front of an audience. "No."

"What?"

"No. I can take them from down here." She tried to look at Bruce, but she was having a hard time just staying on her feet. On the ground, on the floor. She was safe.

"Afraid you'll break a nail?"

"Bruce," Meri yelled from the platform. "She can do them from down there, now let it be."

"She can get them now. Get up there or get out."

Doug frowned at him. "What the hell—"

That was all Geordie heard before she turned and ran from the room. She'd been stupid to think she could make a go of this.

She couldn't work here. Not having to climb ladders and being yelled at by a man who hated her without even knowing her. She reached the annex and threw her camera into her case, snatched up her equipment and ran not toward the kitchen but to the emergency exit at the end of the annex hall. She shot the bolt and fled into the parking lot. One of the trucks was still parked, hiding her car from view.

She made a beeline behind the truck and ducked out of sight just as Meri opened the back door and looked out. Geordie heard the door slam and cautiously looked out from behind the truck.

Meri had gone back inside.

Well, at least Meri had come looking for her.

Geordie threw her equipment into the car and climbed in after it. Fumbled desperately for her keys with shaking fingers.

Damn Bruce. Damn this stupid fear. She finally dragged her keys out of her bag and after several tries, found the ignition. Then she backed out of the lot and drove away without looking back.

"OKAY, WHAT THE hell was that all about?" Doug asked Bruce just as Meri ran back into the foyer.

"She's gone. I checked the annex, the office, the kitchen, her car is gone." She turned on Bruce. "What the heck is wrong with you?"

Carlyn stuck her head around the corner. "What's all the commotion about?"

"Bruce just fired Geordie."

"He can't do that." Carlyn turned to Doug. "He can't do that, can he?"

"No, he can't. What the hell is it with you and that girl?"

Bruce knew he had stepped way over the line. It wasn't even Geordie's fault. It was him. He was tired. Tired of being broke, tired of juggling too many jobs. Of driving an old car that was going to fall apart any minute. Of having to scrape and fight for everything he got. Of being attracted to a woman who wouldn't give him the time of day.

"She only got this assignment because her family are the Holts.

"From the Holt Corporation?" Doug pursed his lips in a silent whisper.

"So?" Meri said.

"So she's a spoiled rich girl out on a lark at our expense."

"That isn't true," Meri said.

"She's been useless and antagonistic since the get-go."

Carlyn raised her eyes to the ceiling. "Maybe you should try kissing her instead of insulting her. She could probably fund this whole project from her clothes allowance."

"Ugh." Meri shoved her hands in her pockets.

Probably to keep from hitting him. Bruce couldn't blame her if she did.

"Is that why you've been on her case since the get-go? Because she's from a rich family?"

"I wasn't."

Meri gave him a look.

"She doesn't know what she's doing."

"So? None of us did when we started. She's a good photographer. With a little guidance, she would know what to do." She stopped to give him another disgusted look. "We always work with newbies."

"But we don't pay them, or at least not a full salary."

"Oh, my Lord." Carlyn threw up her hands and disappeared from the doorway.

"We're budgeted so much for start-up. And her fee is coming out of that." He stopped. "Unless Mommy and Daddy are paying for her to work."

This time Meri threw up her hands. "What does it matter? Now we don't have a photographer. And that puts us behind schedule. And we've barely started. Unless you want to run after her and throw yourself on her mercy, you *dummkopf*."

"She wouldn't even climb the damn scaffolding."

"She's afraid of heights. Yeesh. Where is your brain? No don't answer that." She marched off down the hallway.

Bruce turned to Doug. "Did you know she was afraid of heights?"

Doug shook his head. "But that would explain why she didn't want to climb up the scaffolding."

Bruce shot his hands through his hair. Forced them down by his sides. "Why didn't she say so?"

"Um, you didn't really give her a chance."

"Still it doesn't change the fact that she's a dabbling little rich girl and doesn't know what she's doing."

"Maybe not, but Meri and Carlyn like her, and so far they're the only full-time staff I'm budgeted for. And unless you want to get down on your hands and knees and start stripping wallpaper in between documenting the project and overseeing the repairs and reconstructions, I'd say, we probably want to try and get her back."

Bruce sighed. There was no question as to who Doug

thought should beg Geordie to come back. He rubbed a hand across his face. "Doug, I'm sorry. I don't know what's wrong with me. I'll go apologize. Ask her to come back."

Doug just gave him one of those man-to-man, thank-God-I'm-not-in-your-shoes looks, before he turned and left the room. It didn't make Bruce feel any better that he could hear him muttering to himself as he walked down the hall.

Bruce had jeopardized the project and he didn't even really know that Geordie hadn't gotten the job herself. What was happening to him, to be so vicious?

From the moment he saw her, he'd resented her. Because he'd seen all the things he'd ever aspired to and could never have. It wasn't the money thing. Though who but a pampered rich brat would come to a renovation site driving an expensive sports car and wearing designer clothes?

She was clueless about a lot of things, but not so many as Bruce wanted to accuse her of. She did take a good photo. Even though he could tell her heart wasn't in documentation. She was creative, a free spirit. He'd recognized that, too. And was drawn to it more than he wanted to admit.

So why wasn't she doing what she wanted? Did she even know what she wanted? Bruce had known from high school that he wanted to study architecture. And living in Newport, he took preservation seriously.

He'd put in his time as an intern. An admittance that made him squirm with regret. He hadn't been much younger than Geordie when he volunteered for his first project. He'd screwed up plenty, but instead of putting him down or firing him, the project manager, the conservator and even the assistants had been patient and shown him the ropes. Gave him a chance to succeed.

And how had he repaid their generosity? The first chance he had to do the right thing, he'd lit into a newbie, insulted her every chance he got, and fired her, even though he didn't have the right to fire anyone. It was Doug's project. Bruce was just one of the team.

A team that needed a project photographer. A team that needed Geordie. And he knew it would be up to him to get her back.

But he had no idea where to find her.

Carlyn would have her phone number and home address. He'd start there. No he'd start with an apology to his colleagues, then he'd ask for their help.

Chapter 7

· · · · · · · · · ·

GEORDIE PULLED OUT of the Gilbert House parking area, barely aware of where she was going. She couldn't believe she'd let that jerk trick her into walking out. *Walking out.* She'd just walked out on a job. Even in her most ridiculous attempts at working, she'd never walked out without completing the project or honoring her two-week notice.

But she'd just run out on the most interesting job she'd ever had.

Okay, maybe she didn't love the documentation part. The actual, realistic details didn't rock her world like it did Meri's and Doug's and even Bruce's, damn him. But the other stuff, the photos she got after the initial photographs, the play of light, the distortion of detail, the people caught in an unsuspecting moment, their expressions frozen yet alive, the color modulated by filters or natural light.

That was good stuff. Maybe she was a fake. And the worse

kind, begrudgingly doing their work so she could have some fun with hers. But she'd gotten some dynamite shots.

Unfortunately, dynamite shots did not constitute a career. Maybe she would be better off giving in and joining the corporate office and doing some menial job to fund her "hobby" of photography.

Of course she wouldn't be allowed to do some menial job. She'd be forced into corner-office stuff. Her sister Alicia, who was in marketing, had married a podiatrist just to get out of the family business.

Somehow that seemed like a really unacceptable choice.

About as unacceptable as not being able to climb up a ladder. Why, oh why, had she refused to go back to therapy? Even on the breakers, she'd totally forgotten the techniques that she'd used in the past.

And now she was screwed.

Had her parents really bribed someone to take her on? Had they donated the money for her salary? It was just like something her dad would do.

Her mouth opened into a soundless scream, followed by an ear-piercing bellow of hurt and anger. She pulled to the curb and banged on the steering wheel. The car shuddered in response.

When she finally looked up, she realized she was on Bellevue Avenue, a block from Marble House. One of her favorites. She couldn't imagine it ever being half as neglected as poor Gilbert House.

Gilbert House had fallen on dire times, had been misused and disrespected for decades. And frankly, Geordie didn't see how they would even get it halfway back to where it might have been a century ago.

Well, to hell with it. It was no longer her concern. Let them do their own documentation. Let Bruce climb up that scaffolding and snap a few shots with his phone. Then he'd be sorry.

The thought totally deflated her. They didn't need her. They didn't even want her. Neither Meri nor Carlyn had stood up for her.

Made excuses for me.

"Oh, stop whining." She huffed out the last—hopefully the last—of her anger and hurt. She pulled into the Marble House parking lot, took a camera out of her bag, put the rest of her equipment in the trunk, and struck off across the street to do her own kind of pictures.

She didn't even slow down at the gate of Marble House, just strode up the circular drive, showed her membership card and went inside. She knew she wouldn't be able to take any shots, not with her camera anyway. But she could in her mind. Implanting it on her brain, playing with it in her thoughts. It was a way to train the eye so you didn't miss opportunity when you suddenly came upon a shot.

She walked through the foyer, passing the guided tour offer. She'd been here plenty of times. Loved the steadiness of the architecture, the security of the thick, hard walls tempered by ridiculously ornate decorations.

She tried to imagine the people who had once lived here, died here during the height of the Gilded Age with their reckless making and spending of money. Up and down the avenue year after year, moving between Manhattan and Newport, chasing entertainment, attention, power.

She could almost see them moving around the rooms, ghostly and restless, trapped in a gilded cage, replaying their scandals, their power plays, their triumphs, their failures over and over and over into eternity. The famous and the infamous.

Those people were trapped as surely as if they had been locked inside, dependent on their wealth to make them feel secure. She didn't really want to consider whether she, too, was trapped by her family's wealth. Oh, she could travel and be semi-independent, but she could never get free. Not really. Not yet anyway.

And suddenly she wanted to be free. Break the bonds, breathe fresh ocean air. She retraced her steps and walked straight out the door, earning a strange look from the docent and leaving the old rooms behind. Leaving the ghosts behind. They would still be there the next time she came.

But today she'd had enough of mansions, even beautiful ones. What made them special were the people who'd inhabited them. That's what interested her. Not the ceiling paintings or the Siena marble, not even the tiles hidden beneath the paint layers on the old front steps of Gilbert House.

They didn't speak to her like they did to Meri and Doug and Bruce, even Carlyn, with her background in finance.

So what ignited her passion? Not the hot, hunky guy kind of passion but the soul-deep kind, the kind that would make her spend her life struggling to make ends meet just so she could keep doing what she was doing. Working long, uncomfortable hours only to come back and do it again.

Meri had said it would take months to clean and strip the ceiling. Working through the years of paint layers in increments of inches, not just painting on some solvent and wiping the whole clean. Cataloguing each layer for color and composition, until she came to the first layer of paint. She didn't want to lose one bit of the underneath layers. Because there might be something fabulous there.

Meri couldn't wait to get started.

Geordie wanted to feel that, too. But she'd wrecked any chance she had of finding it at Gilbert House with Doug's crew.

She sat on a bench by the drive, her camera forgotten on her lap. Frowning into space. In limbo.

A butterfly flitted by and landed on a shrub. Geordie didn't care much for photos of butterflies, but she couldn't just sit on a bench all day. So she took a shot. When it swooped to another bush, she stood and took another.

And another, catching it in flight, on a branch. She walked down the path to the lawn until it finally led her to the Chinese tea pagoda, where tourists stopped for refreshments.

It landed on the stone wall where two young girls had taken their sandwiches. Tweenies, Geordie guessed, staying as far away as possible from their parents and little brother, who were sitting at a table across the patio.

When the butterfly landed on the lid of a soda bottle, Geordie was ready, capturing the look of delight in those faces that were trying so hard to be mature. Geordie smiled. She didn't even have to look at the shot to know she nailed it. Had caught them at their most secret, vulnerable moment. Two girls and a butterfly.

The butterfly flew away. The two girls, heads nearly touching, giggled over some shared secret. Four older women who had been having tea at one of the tables got up in a flurry of laughter and conversation. They moved down the path toward the sea, and Geordie moved with them.

They walked slowly, since one of them used a cane and another was supported by the arm of her friend. Geordie could tell they had known one another for a long time.

The four ladies came to the edge of the lawn and stopped to gaze out to the ocean. The cliff walk followed the water below them, tunneling beneath the teahouse before reappearing on the other side. Beyond the walk, the ocean spread out to the sky. Geordie moved closer, keeping the ladies between her and the drop to the cliff walk, and took a few shots of blue.

The expanse of ocean was beautiful, commanding, inspiring, but she'd missed seeing it the day before because she hadn't been able to climb the breakers. The fear was all in her head. She knew that. For all the good it did. It had the power to paralyze her.

She moved closer. The women must have heard her coming up behind them because one of them turned around and smiled.

"Dear, would you mind taking a picture of us?" She held up her camera.

"I'd love to." Geordie moved close enough to take the camera from the woman.

The four of them crowded together.

"On the count of three." Geordie knew that was the surest way to kill spontaneity, but she also knew they would like it.

They did, and when she handed the camera back they thanked her profusely.

As they walked back to the mansion, Geordie called out, "Oh, ladies."

The four of them turned around and Geordie took a series of shots as they laughed, became flustered, and finally settled into that rigid smile that people use to take photos.

"If you'll give me an e-mail address, I'll send you photos. Or I can print some out and send them to you."

"No need. I have a photo printer," the lady with the cane said. She gave Geordie her e-mail addy and with another round of thanks, they walked away.

Geordie watched them go and with them her brief flurry of excitement, which left her feeling bereft and more despondent than ever.

She needed her job back. So what if she didn't know much about architectural documentation? She could learn. And if it wasn't the end all of professions, she might grow to like it. And at least it would be better than waiting tables or working in the corporate office.

But would Bruce hire her back? Had she really gotten the job by herself, or was it like he thought, due to her parents' influence? She'd thought she'd really aced the interview, but maybe she was full of it. Maybe she hadn't gotten the job at all. Maybe . . . She reached for her phone. There was one thing she really needed to know.

Her mother's social secretary answered on the second ring.

"Hi Val, is the lady of the manor at home?"

"Good day, Geordie. If you're looking for your mother, I'll see if she's available." Without waiting for an answer, she put Geordie on hold.

Geordie made a face at the phone. The woman had so sense of humor, no good moods, actually no bad moods that Geordie could remember. She was an automaton. The only sane way to work for the Holt family.

Her mother's voice came on a few minutes later. Before she could ask Geordie how her job was going, Geordie asked her own question.

"Of course he didn't," her mother said. "If your father was inclined to pay anything it would be for them not to hire you. You know how stubborn he is." A sigh that whooshed over the phone. "I suppose it's my fault."

"Your fault?"

"For giving him three girls instead of a son to take over the business."

Geordie looked up at Marble House. The Victorian "cottage" was a perfect setting for her mother's attitude about women, a totally different era—at least a hundred years behind the times. Never mind that Alva Vanderbilt had held suffragette meetings in the teahouse before leaving Newport for good.

"Actually I was half Dad's fault."

"Not you, darling. You weren't a fault. Anyway, you got that job on your own and should be very proud. How are you liking it?"

I got fired after four days. "Fine. I'm really liking it. Interesting and challenging."

"Oh, I'm so glad." Her mother's relief was palpable. "You'll have to come to dinner one night when your father and I are both here. God knows when that will be. I'll put Val on and you can ask her to put you on the calendar."

She had to make an appointment with her parents through the social secretary. Surely this wasn't normal. "I will, but I'll have to call her back later. We're pretty busy at work right now. I'll see when I can get off."

They said their good-byes and hung up. Geordie returned the phone to her pocket.

It was almost six and the grounds would be closing soon. She'd spent the whole day here following butterflies and strangers, when she should have been at work with the others.

She must have been out of her mind to walk out like that. She *had* been out of her mind.

And she'd have to do something to rectify her temporary insanity. Because if it was a choice between facing her parents knowing that she was again career-less or standing up to Bruce Stafford and making him take her back, it would go to the cranky architect.

But she couldn't approach him with things the way they were now. And she couldn't challenge him when she was still land bound.

No. She would do what she needed to do . . . somehow. She'd get up that scaffolding one way or the other. Then he'd have no reason for not taking her back.

She would do it now, before she had time to talk herself out of it.

Chapter 8

. . . .

IT WAS AFTER six when Bruce finally gave up looking for Geordie. The only thing he hadn't done was call her parents' house. Somehow he didn't think she would want them to know that she was AWOL.

He was hungry, tired, and beginning to feel a little panicky. If she was afraid of heights, what other things might she be afraid of? Were there other phobias? Just how fragile was she?

Surely she wouldn't do anything drastic just because he'd been a little rude to her. Okay, more than rude.

They'd all been excited and anxious to begin and had left her to figure out things by herself. They wouldn't have done that with an intern. And he'd been particularly mean to her.

He didn't know why she brought that out in him. Or if it even had anything to do with her at all.

God, he'd made a mess of it.

He found himself driving past Gilbert House, made a sharp turn and pulled into the parking lot. Maybe someone was still there, had heard from her or had an idea where to look next.

But everyone else had called it a day; the lot was empty . . . except for one little sports car.

Damn. Had she been here the whole time while he'd been searching all over Newport for her? Why hadn't someone called him? And where was everybody else? Surely they wouldn't have left her to lock up by herself. Bruce was willing to give her another chance, but he didn't trust her with the security of the building and he couldn't believe Doug would either.

He pulled up to the back entrance. Jumped out and tried the door. It was locked. He rifled through his keys and unlocked it. It was dark in the hallway and in the kitchen. She must be in the annex.

Maybe Doug had already hired her back and Bruce could get by with a quick apology. But she wasn't in the annex. The room was dark. He stood in the doorway, listening. Nothing overhead.

Should he check her car? He would have seen her if she was sitting there. So help him, if she had been out at the local pub with Meri and Carlyn while he spent the day looking for her, he would be pissed.

He took a breath. No he wouldn't. His temper had caused enough trouble for one day. Now he was sorry. And worried.

He retraced his steps and was about to return to the kitchen when he heard something. He turned and walked into the foyer. It was dark, the scaffolding was barely discernible in the dying light.

A choked cry.

What the hell? He looked around, then up. Didn't understand what he was seeing for a good three seconds. Then it hit him all at once.

Geordie was three quarters up the scaffolding, her body plastered to the frame, her hands clenched around the rungs.

"Geordie?"

She didn't answer. Didn't even acknowledge him.

"Look, I'm sorry. I was out of line."

Nothing.

"Geordie, come down. You don't have to do this."

A spasmodic jerk of her head.

"Are you all right? Are you hurt?"

No response.

"Okay, just hold on. I'm coming up."

He started to climb; the scaffolding was firm but it vibrated with his first step, and he heard her swallowed cry. He stepped more gently, at least he tried. His pulse was racing, his mouth was dry. What if she had fallen? What if he'd startled her and she fell when he was trying to help? What if she resented him seeing her stuck up the scaffolding like a cat up a tree?

He climbed until he stood a rung lower and reached for her back. His touch only made her press harder against the pipes.

He placed his hands on the bars on either side of her, effectively trapping her there. "I won't let you fall. Let go and I'll help you down."

Still no response, but being this close he felt her body convulsing. She was shaking so hard that the scaffolding rattled.

"Come on, Just one hand. Let go."

Another one of those spasmodic jerks of her head. He reached up and enclosed one of her hands in his. It felt tiny and delicate. He tried to gently pry it loose from the bars. But her grip was strong; panic had frozen her fingers around the rung.

What did he do now? Climb down? Call the fire department? He tried to reach in his pocket for his cell. But her hand came away with his and she fell back, nearly causing him to lose his balance—and hers.

He gave up the phone idea. Wrapped his free arm around her waist. Pulled her close. She was still shaking so violently that for a minute he was afraid she might knock them both down.

But he managed to drag her down one rung, though one hand still clung to the bar. He stepped down one more and pulled her with him. The hand came away, but she was stiff, stuck in that half crouch like she was still clinging to the ladder.

It was like carrying a manikin.

Until he reached the ground. He pulled her away from the scaffold. He tried to set her on her feet, but she went boneless and he just managed to throw his other arm around her waist before she slipped from his grip.

She was still shaking violently and he really didn't have a clue as to what to do.

"It's okay. It's okay." It was all he could think of to say.

It wasn't okay. What had possessed her to come back and climb the damn thing? How did she even get inside? Surely Doug hadn't given her a key.

They were standing melded together, her back to his front and he didn't think she had a clue as to where she was or who she was with. He turned her around, meaning to take her by the shoulders and get her to pull herself together. But her eyes were clamped shut and as soon as she faced him, she grabbed the front of his shirt in a death grip. He pulled her close, patted her back, smoothed her crop of short hair.

She was a nice fit but he was feeling anything but amorous. "Geordie. Open your eyes; you're on the ground. You're safe." He spoke as soothingly as he could, though he felt like yelling, *You idiot, what do you think you were trying to prove?*

She sucked in a harsh breath, the shaking became slower and less violent.

"How long were you stuck up there?"

She shook her head.

"A long time?"

"Wh-what time is it?"

"Nearly eight o'clock."

A ragged laugh. "An hour."

"Jesus."

She turned her head away, her eyes squeezed tight.

"Look at me." He tilted her chin up. "Look at me."

Finally her eyelids fluttered open. "Sorry. I'll leave now." She pulled away and her knees gave way.

Bruce pulled her even closer. It was easier to say what he had to say over the top of her head. "Look. I don't want you to go. I just let my own shit get in the way of my judgment. It didn't have anything to do with you."

Except that it did, because her lack of experience and her rich-girl status weren't the only things that bugged him about her. As they stood in the center of the foyer, glommed together, the danger past, he recognized what he was feeling.

In civilized terms he was attracted to her. In a man's terms, he wanted her. And he wanted her bad.

Which was not happening. Still, as she relaxed into his arms, he couldn't stop himself from running his cheek along her hair. It was soft and straight and feathery. He kissed the top of her head.

She pulled away. "I'm okay now. I'm so stupid. I should have told you why I couldn't go up the scaffolding. I just . . . I wasn't expecting to have to go up. It just took me by surprise."

She tried to move away but he held her close. He wasn't quite ready to let her go. "No, I jumped to the wrong conclusion. I do that a lot." He smiled down at her and was flooded by unexpected warmth when she smiled back at him, though it was a smile tempered with disbelief. "I've been looking for you all day."

She looked up then. Really looked at him. "Why?"

"I told you. I was out of line. You're a good photographer."

"Just not good at documentation."

"You can learn. If you still want to. If you want to come back to work."

"You mean I'm not fired?"

The hopeful look on her face nearly broke his heart. It was weird. He'd never seen a vulnerable side from her. Had not even guessed she had one.

"Well?"

"Actually, I didn't have the authority to fire you. Only Doug does, and he read me good for stepping over the line. So please, come back. And save my bacon."

"What about . . . ?" She jerked her head toward the foyer.

"You don't have to climb any ladders. Meri can do those shots."

"No. It's part of the job. And if I can't do the job—"

"To hell with the job." And now he said what he'd been thinking all along. "What the hell were you trying to prove by going up there? You could have been hurt, you could have broken your damn neck. God knows what."

"I know, irresponsible. I get it. I said I was sorry. You should have left me up there."

He let go of pent-up breath. "Good to see you're getting back to normal."

"I would have been fine, but I missed lunch and I just got a little light-headed."

"Fine. You can try again. But not now. Right now I'm taking you to get something to eat."

"I'll just get something at home."

"Then I'm driving you."

"But my car."

"I'll drive it over."

"What about your car?"

"I'll come back for it later."

"You don't have to."

"I don't have to. But I want to." He needed to make amends. And besides he wasn't in a hurry to leave her.

She began to recover quickly, too quickly; he was rather enjoying holding on to her. By the time he'd locked the exterior door, she was walking on her own and headed for her car. He hurried to catch up. He didn't trust her not to jump in her car and drive away without him.

And he did have a few questions, starting with, "How did you get in? Was Doug still here?"

She shook her head.

"He gave you a key?"

Another head shake.

"Then how?"

"I left by the emergency exit by the annex. I guess it didn't lock." She flinched as if she thought he was going to yell at her.

Until a few minutes ago, he would have. But he let it pass. He was pretty sure she wouldn't be doing that again.

"I'd better go make sure it's locked now."

"It is. I made sure to lock it when I went inside. But check it if you don't trust me."

She stopped by the driver's side of her car. Waited. He really wanted to make sure it was locked, but he'd have to take her word for it. The situation was fragile at best. He could come back later and double-check, once he'd made sure she had something to eat.

He shook his head and held out his hand. "Keys?"

She hesitated.

"Don't trust me?"

She begrudgingly reached into her jeans pocket and pulled out a key ring. Handed it to him and walked around to the other side of the car.

They didn't talk except when she gave him directions. She seemed really reluctant to—maybe she didn't want him to see where she lived. God, maybe she lived with her parents, or with her boyfriend? Which would be worse?

And what the hell was he thinking. He'd given her a hard time all week and was suddenly wondering what her social life was like? He must have been breathing in too much lead paint.

"You can stop at the next corner. I can park the car."

He gave her a look.

"I'm fine really."

"Glad to hear it, but I'm driving your car and I'm seeing you into your apartment. And making sure you eat something." One look at her face and he changed tack. "We'll order out. Or we can go out. But either way, I'm not leaving you until you're safely inside for the night. And in case you think I'm just being a control freak, well, I am. Can't help it. And besides, you scared the crap out of me."

"Sorry." She sighed heavily. "Okay, but I have my job back, right?"

"Yes. Why?"

"Turn right at the next corner."

They were down by the wharf. Prime real estate.

"Left into the parking lot."

Of course. Waterfront condos. Luxury building. She didn't even need this job. What the hell was she doing working in restoration? A hobby? She never needed to climb a ladder again. What was the deal?

He parked the car in the allotted spot.

Geordie got out and started walking toward the entrance of the complex. She waved her key card at the electronic reader and stepped inside.

He stepped in right behind her.

She cut him a sideways look, then walked straight to an elevator, pressed the button, and stared at the doors until they opened and she stepped inside. He stepped in with her.

She glared up at him. "Just so you know. This is not my apartment. I'm just staying here until . . ." She trailed off.

Until what, he wondered? He was beginning to feel uncomfortable. He didn't belong in a building like this. He was dirty from poking around the old house, then scouring the town to find her.

Geordie looked like she'd been through hell and back.

He had to admit he liked her better this way.

The doors opened and he followed her down a hall, waited while she unlocked the door and stepped inside. The first thing he saw was the lights of the harbor. Not too shabby.

She turned on the lights.

It was white, sleek, open concept. Sterile and cold. She dropped her keys on the granite kitchen counter, walked to the Sub-Zero fridge and looked inside. "I have bottled water and Moët Chandon."

"I'm fine."

She took out a bottle of water, opened it and guzzled half of it.

"I guess you're not going to forgive me without making me suffer a little, are you?"

She snorted and nearly choked on her water.

"You're an enigma, Geordie Holt."

"No I'm not. I'm a mess. You just noticed faster than most people."

She continued through the space, turning on lights. Came to a dimmer switch and light flooded the apartment. White, white walls, white couch, white drapes, white desk, glass tables.

And set in a line, propped up along one wall were photographs, some in color, some in black-and-white. They were all the color and design the place needed.

There were landscapes, still lifes, and abstract designs, but it was the portraits that caught his attention. Young and old, beautiful and ugly, sad, happy, pensive. Words didn't come close to describing what he was seeing. The nuances of their expressions, their feelings and thoughts just out of reach, their lives outside of the camera. She'd captured them all. This was the last thing he'd expected.

"Damn, Geordie. These are amazing."

Chapter 9

· · · · · · · · ·

GEORDIE WATCHED BRUCE bend down to look more closely at one of her photographs. She particularly liked the one he'd zeroed in on. A child holding an empty ice-cream cone, the ice cream—lime sherbet—melting at his feet.

In another photographer's hand it might have been maudlin. But not in hers. She'd managed to capture that moment of surprise, the instant before surprise turned to heartbreak. She was proud of it and she was happy that Bruce had recognized it, too.

Well, his taste had never been in question. Just his attitude.

And maybe he had his own issues. He'd pretty much admitted he was a control freak. Well, surprise. But at least he'd admitted it. There was hope.

For him maybe, but what about for her? What the hell was she going to do if she couldn't even climb up twenty feet?

Bruce stood. "Are all of them yours?"

Geordie shrugged, then nodded slightly. Almost as if she didn't want to claim them. And that was crazy. She was proud of them. They were her best work. And if no one else took her seriously . . . And there it was. She turned away.

"They're really good."

"Good doesn't pay the rent. Which is why I'm living in a corporate apartment that belongs to my father's business." And why if she didn't get this right, she'd be working in that same business so she could afford half this apartment.

And speaking of rent . . . the envelope with her father's check was still lying on the counter. Damning evidence of Geordie's inability to stand on her own two feet. She opened the drawer and slid it off the counter and out of sight.

Besides she didn't need to afford this apartment. She didn't want this apartment. Or one like it. She just wanted . . . What did she want?

She walked to the balcony, slid the doors open, letting the night air pour in.

Bruce stood where she'd left him. But now he was watching her instead of looking at her photos. What was his deal? Why didn't he leave?

She supposed she'd have to feed him to thank him for dragging her down from that damn scaffolding. Great impression. He'd probably tell the whole crew that she was afraid of heights. That she was totally useless unless they needed details at ground level.

She lived three stories up, standing inside the doorway to the balcony. The sky was filled with stars, the harbor lights mimicking their light, and she was afraid to go out. A few months ago she could have stepped across that threshold. Not close to the edge, maybe, but she could stand outside the doorway. She could sit on one of the chairs and drink her morning coffee.

But now . . . She closed the door, rested her forehead against the cool glass.

She'd have to go back to therapy. Start the whole process again, because she couldn't live like this.

She felt Bruce come to stand right behind her. "Do you want me to go? Or can I buy you dinner?"

She was so tempted just to lean back, let him feed her, let him decide on the restaurant, let him pay, let him . . . and that's where life always ended up. Someone else taking care of her.

"We can order in. I'm too dirty and tired to go out. And I'll pay. Actually I'll put it on the expense account." She held up her hand. "In case you're wondering if I always live like this, the answer is . . ." She hesitated. "The answer is yes, more or less." She looked at him and said the last thing she would ever tell anyone. "I just haven't figured out how not to."

"I GUESS YOU think I'm pretty spoiled," Geordie said spooning pad Thai onto the apartment's white china. "And you'd be right. But in my defense it's not all it's cracked up to be."

They'd opened the bottle of champagne, and Bruce poured more into her glass. "It sounds pretty good to me."

"Yeah, it sounds good. And it definitely has perks, but it exacts a price."

"Like going to work for your father?"

"Yeah. My other two sisters got away. My mother said it was her fault for not having boys."

Bruce wrinkled his eyebrows.

"I know. Gothic. But at least she said my father didn't make someone give me this job. I called her today and asked her. So you can stop thinking that."

Bruce acknowledged the hit with a tip of his chin. A pretty nice looking chin.

Geordie laughed. "That doesn't mean my mother didn't put the screws to somebody. But I didn't think to ask her that. I should move to Antarctica."

"Have you ever thought about standing up to them?"

"Yes and I do. All the time. They just don't hear me, then they bankroll me in some project that catches my fancy, and I'm right back where I started. But this was going to be the time I really made the break." She laughed. A hollow sound that she didn't like. "So far it isn't working out so great."

Bruce reached for the carton of panang curry. "Well it could. If you took a class or two—"

Geordie burst out laughing. "Sorry, but I'm a serial college student, I've taken classes forever. I know a little about a lot."

"Okay, but listen. If you took a couple of courses to familiarize yourself with restoration, you could do that as your day job, and get together a portfolio for a gallery show."

"You make it sound so simple."

"No, I don't think it will be simple. But at least you might end up doing what you like."

"And starve while doing it."

"Damn it, Geordie, have a little backbone."

"You don't understand."

"No I don't. I've had to fight for everything I've done."

"Which is why you're so uptight." It was a mean thing to say. But really who was he to be casting first stones?

"Which is why I'm so uptight. I know it. This is a particularly difficult time. But at least I'm doing what I want to do. Most of the time."

"But you actually do real work. Not *a-a-art*."

"I do real work, but you haven't seen it. Just this week I signed off on a kitchen renno and fought over tile color with a woman who can't make up her mind. Who I might add hasn't paid me in three months. So I kind of understand not being able to get away. I left the firm I was working with so I could do more restoration work, and now I'm doing bathrooms and closets to make ends meet. But it's worth it." He stopped, frowned at her. "The question is . . . Is it worth it to you?"

Was it? Did she care enough about her photography, *her* photography to risk everything? She could go through life like she had been doing. Taking her family's money and not giving anything in return while they waited for her to grow up and come to work for them. Or get married to someone who could support her while she became her mother, doing charities and garden clubs, and lots of reading.

And somehow, even Geordie the indecisive couldn't go that far. She looked over the pad Thai at Bruce, whose look hadn't wavered. *Is it worth it?* He was still waiting for an answer and she wasn't sure she had one.

"I don't know how to do bathrooms and kitchens."

He stood up. "You're a piece of work, you know that? People who have less than nothing at least have the courage to go after their dream. At least have the courage *to* dream. Most of us aren't given a free meal ticket." He moved away from the table, walked to the sliding doors and peered out. "If those people had a third of your ability and the means to accomplish it, they would go after what they wanted like there was no tomorrow. Not wasting their time, energy, and money waffling from one distraction to another."

He grabbed the handle and yanked the door along the track. Then stepped out into the night.

Geordie pushed her plate away. She wanted to yell at him, tell him to get out, that he couldn't invite himself to dinner and then bitch at her. But she couldn't. Because he was right.

Instead she gathered up the left-over food and took it back to the kitchen. Put the food in the fridge and their dishes in the dishwasher.

Was it worth it to her to give up everything she had to pursue photography? She had never thought about it in those terms before. Not until coming to work at Gilbert House. Meeting and getting to know Meri and Carlyn and Doug. And Bruce.

And not for the first time, she felt paralyzed. The same way she had felt clinging to that scaffolding a few hours before. The same way she felt whenever she'd tried to face a fear, and she had plenty of them.

She walked halfway across the room. Stopped.

Bruce was a mere silhouette against the lights of the harbor. He'd dug right through her good-time facade to the real source of her indecision. Fear.

But she recognized the same fear in him. And a little bitterness. He'd given up his safe life and risked everything for what he loved. She knew that just as surely as if he'd told her.

He was challenging her to do the same. But she wasn't sure she was as strong as he was.

Then again, she bet he didn't have parents he could run back to, contrite after another false start, who would take him back into the fold—at a price. She wasn't sure that comfort was something she could live without. But she did know that she couldn't keep living the way she was.

She stood for a second, then took a step toward the balcony. And another until she was standing on the threshold. Bruce's hands were braced on the railing and he was leaning out looking at the dark water. She knew it though she couldn't see it.

She immediately began to recoil. She wanted to say *Get back from the edge.* The railing may break, the balcony might crumble, you might lose your balance and fall. The world might spiral out of control and you'll be all alone.

He wasn't aware of her. Didn't hear as she stepped across the track and onto the hard flagstone. Didn't turn when she stepped beside him, rose up on tiptoe and kissed his cheek.

Slowly his arm slid around her waist and he pulled her to

his side. She felt safe but she knew she couldn't depend on him any more than she could continue to depend on her parents for her security.

It was time to let go and face her life, whatever it would be.

"You know," Bruce said, still staring out at the water. "Nobody gets along in this world by themselves. But you do have to take the first steps and be willing to sacrifice when the time comes."

"You're pretty wise for a wise guy," Geordie said, not looking at him.

"No, I just know this from experience."

"Do you ever get scared?"

He laughed quietly. "Most of the time."

"It isn't very comfortable."

"But it's never boring." He eased her away from the railing, before she'd realized how close they'd been standing. With his arm still around her, Bruce guided her back into the apartment.

Geordie felt a little disappointed because she knew what was coming next. The same thing that always happened. It was standard dating scenario, though this hadn't exactly been a date. Dinner, talk, roving hands, kissing, bed. She could feel his attraction to her. She felt the same toward him. And yet . . .

When they were back in the living room, Bruce put both hands on her arms. She lifted her face to him.

But he turned her around to face her row of photographs and moved close behind her. "Think about what you're going to do with all of these."

She felt his breath on the back of her neck, felt the beginning thrill as his lips touched her neck.

"You'd better get some sleep. You don't want to be late for work. Thanks for dinner."

He dropped his hands and walked toward the door.

She watched him, wondering what had just happened.

"You know, you just stood out on your balcony. You weren't even scared. Were you?" He closed the door behind him.

Geordie stared at the closed door. Then slowly she began to smile. By the time she turned out the lights the smile had turned to a grin.

Chapter 10

· · · · · · · · · ·

GEORDIE DROVE INTO the Gilbert House parking lot early the next morning. She wanted to catch Meri and Carlyn before the others arrived and as she'd hoped the only cars in the lot belonged to the two women. She breathed a huge sigh of relief, but that relief began to desert her as she walked across the asphalt, turned the knob, stepped in the hall. What if they were fed up with her?

She heard them before she saw them. "Di-di-di-di-di ban ba ba bon . . . blue-oo moon . . ."

Geordie smiled. How could they not take her back, two grown women who sang sixties songs before work?

She hurried past the kitchen to Carlyn's office.

Meri and Carlyn stood side by side, each sketching a circle in the air with two fingers. Without breaking the rhythm, Meri pulled Geordie into the room, sliding her camera bag off her shoulder and placing it on the desk. Then she positioned Geordie between them and bumped her hip. Carlyn bumped from the other side.

And that's where Doug and Bruce found them a few minutes later, shimmying as the *di di dit dits* died slowly into silence.

Geordie stood up abruptly, her cheeks flooding with heat. Damn. Just when she should be convincing them of her professionalism, they had caught her goofing off. It might be okay for Meri and Carlyn, but she hadn't earned the right to goof off—she hadn't even earned the right to have the job.

"Well," Carlyn said, slouching into one hip and pointing to the two men. "It's a good thing Geordie can sing, or we were going to have draft one of you two tone-deaf Neanderthals into singing with us tomorrow night."

Bruce's face had settled into an expression that was somewhere between confused and amused.

Doug threw both hands in the air. "Thank God for that. Meeting in ten minutes, kitchen. I'll make the coffee."

"God, no. I'll make it." Carlyn sprinted out of the room.

Doug smiled smugly. "I get her every time." He followed her out, Bruce close behind.

Meri shut the door behind them. "We've got ten minutes, what happened yesterday? Did Bruce find you? He's really sorry."

Geordie concentrated on getting a camera out of her bag.

"Come on, we don't have all day."

Geordie turned around to face her. "He found me." A stupid giggle escaped. "Stuck up the scaffolding like an idiot. I—I—"

"You're afraid of heights. I got that the day at the beach. You should have just said so. It's no big deal."

"Yeah it is. How can I do my job—"

"Geordie, we're all afraid of something."

"What are you afraid of?"

"Me?" Meri frowned, then shrugged. "I guess . . . well, everything has worked out so great for me. I have a great family, a job that I love, love, love, friends, and wonderful boyfriend. I'm so lucky, but sometimes, I just get this moment of *What if I lost it all?* What would I do? Who would I be?"

"But you wouldn't lose it all."

"No, not all of it, at least not all at once. My dad died before I was born, then Mom met Dan Hollis and I got a new dad and I have three half brothers. When my mom died, I had Gran and Dad and the boys, and Alden next door, and all this. Now Peter is talking about getting married. Sometimes I'm afraid it's too good to be true."

Meri laughed. "But that's not like a real fear, like fear of heights or facing death."

Facing death. It made fear of heights seem irrational, inconsequential, and yet rational thought had nothing to do with irrational fear.

"So I take it he found you and got you down."

Geordie nodded.

"And?"

"He took me home—I mean to my apartment, and ordered food, then said I wasn't fired and he'd see me tomorrow."

Meri quirked an eyebrow. "That sounds promising. Sort of."

Geordie erupted in a surprised laugh. "And he didn't even try to sleep with me."

"Did you want him to?"

"No. I mean I like him okay, when he isn't ranting at me. But I've spent way too long in a scene where hello and a drink always ends in sex. It was such a relief." She lifted one shoulder. "It sort of made me like him better."

Carlyn skidded around the corner and into the room. "What did I miss?"

"Bruce didn't sleep with Geordie."

"Yikes, did you want him to?"

Geordie threw a panicked look toward the open door. "No." *Not yet anyway.*

"Don't worry. They're in there squabbling over whether to gut the upstairs bedrooms first or the downstairs parlor. And want me to come up with enough money to hire two crews. Hah!" She turned to Geordie. "Shoestring Budgets R Us. I think if we ever had one full crew, we'd swallow our tongues, turn blue and pass out. Then nothing would ever get done."

Geordie narrowed her eyes at Carlyn. Was she hinting that Geordie's family could finance the whole project? They probably could. But Geordie wasn't going to ask them.

"Well, I don't care what they do," Meri said. "I spent yesterday running a thorough inspection of my ceiling and plan to start pulling samples today."

"That's what I told them. So, Geordie, are you coming back to work for real?"

"Bruce said I wasn't fired."

"Bruce couldn't fire you anyway. And if he tries to bully

you anymore, I'll give him what for." Carlyn snapped her teeth together, a gesture so at odds with her bubbly personality that Meri and Geordie laughed.

"We'd better get hopping before they drink all the coffee. Oh, did Meri explain that part of the job description is Friday nights at the karaoke bar?"

"Blue-oo moo-oo-oon." Carlyn and Meri danced out the doorway.

Geordie grabbed a camera and her laptop and followed them out.

THE DAY WENT quickly. When she wasn't needed as a photographer, Geordie pitched in to help the others. She and Carlyn rearranged the office to accommodate a giant file cabinet, then collated a list of possible donors. Bagged samples of paint that Meri lowered in a bucket from the top of the scaffolding and organized them in a metal file box that would be carried to the lab for analysis.

Bruce took off around lunchtime to work another job, and Doug went to lunch with a colleague who could potentially loan them several interns. Geordie, Meri, and Carlyn ate deli sandwiches sitting on the back steps, since Meri was covered with dirt, dust, and paint chips; smelled like something astringent; and didn't want to change just to go out for food.

Geordie crunched into a pickle spear and chewed slowly. "Bruce said I should sign up for some courses."

Meri rolled her eyes. "I think you've nailed the photography part."

"How to recognize different architectural details and stuff like that.. Do you know of any?"

"Yeah, there are lot of online classes."

"I've read a lot online already."

"There is nothing wrong with your photos. You'd probably do better to take some basic architecture history classes. So you know what to look for. But do you even like architecture?"

"Sure."

"Seems to me," Carlyn said, crumpling her sandwich paper and putting it back in the bag. "You are more inspired by people than wood and stone."

"Well . . ." Geordie thought about it. Carlyn was right. She'd been at Marble House yesterday, and though she couldn't take interior shots, there were thousands of exterior details to shoot, and most photographers would have a field day with the teahouse. But Geordie had spent her time watching teenage girls, butterflies, and four women tourists.

She couldn't just keep jumping from one thing to another. She put down her sandwich. Wiped off her hands. Told Carlyn and Meri about her father's ultimatum. "I can never settle down to one thing. My parents have had it with me. I tried studio art. My sketching was lousy, my sculpting was worse, so I got into photography. Had a couple of successes at student shows, but didn't get a blink from any of the professional galleries.

"I thought maybe journalism. Worked a few months for a local paper. God, it was boring and they cropped my photos any way they wanted just to fit them between type and advertisements. Besides, newspapers are going the way of all printed matter.

"And I wanted to have control." *And wasn't that the truth?* "At least have a say in what I photograph. Then I thought I would do fashion photography. I mean you're there with the model. Looking for something special, finding it and pulling it out of them, or discovering something different, working with them to get the perfect look. but everything was so . . . editorial, getting the right "Look." It was all put out there rather than discovered. I was more interested in . . . I don't know."

"Regular people?" Meri suggested.

"Well, yeah. But what kind of job is that? Weddings. Birthday parties? Living out of my car and transporting prints from street fair to street fair?"

"Why not?" Meri asked.

"If that's what it takes," Carlyn said.

"Can you just see my dad? Well, you don't know him. But he'd have a fit."

Both women just looked at her.

"He would kick me out of the apartment."

Still just looked.

"How would I survive?"

"The way the rest of us do."

Geordie slumped back. "How do you do it?"

"Well, first," Meri said. "You have to be firm with your parents. My dad was great. Ready to help me out in any way he could, make the path easier, but he knew I had to stand on my own two feet first, before I could accept his help. He did that with the boys, too. And Carlyn had to work her way through school."

"I'm still paying off student loans. I'll probably take some to the grave."

"But you could pay them off faster if you worked in finance."

"Yeah, but I don't want to. I'm doing what I want to do." Carlyn made a face. "Meri's fault. She got me hooked."

"And Carlyn got me hooked on karaoke."

"Now we're stuck with each other."

"Side by side," they both sang.

They were so goofy, but Geordie was a little envious. She'd never had a friend as close as they were. She wondered if she ever would. And would ever have the courage to follow her passion instead of what she knew was rational and expected. When her "dilettantism," as her mother called it, would turn into an avocation.

She had a feeling photography was the one. It's what she always came back to, always took with her. She just had to figure out a way to say no, to be willing to fail, to face whatever she had to face to make it work. And if it didn't work? Well, hell, Meri had said she was afraid of what the future might hold. Everyone with a brain was a little afraid. It kept you on your toes.

"Just make a start."

"Uh-oh," Meri broke in. "You'd better say something quick or Carlyn is going to really start singing. And then, alas, I'll have to join in. And of course we'll expect you . . ."

"Okay, okay. I'm going to do some serious soul searching."

"When?"

"Starting tonight. Now, let's get back to work. There's something I want to do before the guys get back."

They went inside and Geordie led the way past the kitchen, past the office, and into the foyer.

Carlyn grabbed at her sleeve. "Holy cow, Geordie. You don't have to do this."

"You said make a start." She glanced back at them, her breath already beginning to hitch just thinking about what she was about to do. The sweat beginning to collect in her armpits.

"Are you sure?" Meri came to stand next to Geordie.

Geordie nodded; she wasn't sure she could talk.

"Oh hell," Carlyn came up to her other side. "Just so you know. I hate climbing almost as much as I hate stinky."

"You don't have to," Geordie breathed out.

"Neither do you. On the count of three."

"One."

Geordie concentrated on the rung in front of her face. Put an image of a calming ocean in her mind. Counted to five for each breath. In, out, in, out.

"Two."

She licked her lips. It was now or never. She'd done the therapy. She knew what to do. Focus, concentrate on her safe place. She'd managed before. She'd just been stupid last night. She could do this.

"Three."

She would do this.

Beside her Meri and Carlyn put a foot on the first rung and each laid an encouraging hand on her back.

Geordie pushed her foot to the first rung. It felt a heavy and sluggish, but finally it settled on the rung. She felt the other two women shift weight and they had both feet on the scaffolding.

Geordie lifted her other foot. She could hear Carlyn humming "Side by Side" under her breath. It was such a cornball thing to do. The kind of thing a few weeks ago, Geordie would have made fun of. Scoffed at.

She was grateful for it now. Beside her, Meri joined the song and they climbed another rung. And another. Somewhere in their ascent Geordie added her voice to theirs. It was breathy and wobbly but it was there and it got her to the top.

She didn't stand but sat at the edge of the platform between Meri and Carlyn, not daring to look down.

Until a voice below them exclaimed, "What the hell?"

She did look down then, and the world started to spin.

Meri and Carlyn each put an arm around her.

"Go away," Meri yelled.

But Bruce just stood there.

"Now!" Carlyn said.

Bruce backed up, his eyes on Geordie and she realized she was looking back and she wasn't dizzy.

And then he was gone; she closed her eyes.

Chapter 11

· · · · · · · · · ·

"Now that we're up here," Meri said. "Look up at my ceiling."

Geordie opened her eyes and looked up. She still had to concentrate on breathing slowly, and she still felt a little shaky, but she looked at the dingy ceiling and wondered what Meri was seeing that excited her so much.

"Can you see it?"

"Your ceiling?"

"No. That."

Geordie couldn't see anything but ugly paint.

Meri stood up, making the scaffolding vibrate. Geordie clutched at the wood she was sitting on.

"Look," Meri said pointing to a crack in the paint. "I cheated a little. It wasn't my fault some of the paint flaked off and there is a small line. Which might be, just might be . . . something important." She shrugged.

"Don't mind her, she tends to get carried away."

Meri did seem a little excitable. What could she possibly expect to see in that less-than-an-inch square of something that looked just as muddy as the first layer of paint?

And then a revelation hit her so forcibly that she almost forgot to be afraid. Whatever Meri was seeing was the same thing Geordie saw when looking through a lens. She squinted at the ceiling, but it still looked dingy and murky eggplant gray.

"Can you tell what's underneath?" she asked.

"Nope. We can't afford any X-ray equipment, just like we can't afford a hydraulic lift, hence the scaffolding." She gestured to the wooden planks that stretched almost wall-to-wall.

There were two moveable platforms set at opposite ends of the platform. "What are those for?"

Meri grimaced. "For when I can't reach a place standing and have to lie on my back."

Geordie wrinkled her nose at the prospect.

"Sort of like Michelangelo at the Sistine Chapel." Meri grinned.

Geordie cast another upward look. "What if there's nothing underneath all that paint but more ugly paint?"

"Oh, there will be."

"Are you sure?"

"Hell, Geordie, no one knows anything for sure," Carlyn said.

That was true if Geordie's life up to this point was any indication.

"But Doug has a sixth sense for diamonds in the rough," Meri said.

"Though this is a little rougher than usual," Carlyn added.

"Do you always work for Doug?"

"As much as I can," Meri said. "Sometimes I work on other projects. Actually I'm kind of in demand. But my loyalty is to Doug."

"What about you, Carlyn?"

"So far just for Doug. It's the kind of thing where you build a relationship with your colleagues, and with the donors, too. Now, they only run sometimes when they see me coming."

"And Bruce?"

"He's come in a few times for consults, but this is the first time he's been in at the beginning."

"Kind of wound tight," Carlyn said.

"He could probably give you some insight into the job thing," Meri said. "He just went solo so he could spend more time doing restoration work. I think he's having a little trouble making ends meet."

Carlyn wagged a finger, Motown style. "But don't let him bum you out."

"Big chip on his shoulder," Meri added.

"Yeah, I got that. Though . . ." Geordie thought about his reaction to her photos the night before, how he'd relaxed and talked about his work and hers as they ate, how he slipped his arm around her when she came to the balcony. A gesture of security, understanding, maybe.

"Though what?" Carlyn asked.

"Nothing. I don't know."

"You want me to try and line you up some other jobs? We do most of our own documentation except at the beginning and end of a project. Freelancing is satisfying but it takes some juggling to be working all the time."

"I know. I'm not sure I can do it."

Meri shifted her weight. "Well, only you can figure it out, but we're here to listen. But right now, I have to get to work." She slid her feet to the rungs.

"You coming?"

Geordie made a face. "Funny."

BRUCE STOOD AT the kitchen counter, feeling like his heart was caught in his throat. He'd seen Geordie sitting up on that scaffolding with a mixture of anxiety, relief, and a little jealousy that she'd managed it with Meri and Carlyn and not him. Which was totally ridiculous.

But he'd imagined himself helping her over her phobia like some knight in slightly tarnished armor. Like he didn't have enough to worry about. At least his client had finally settled on tile for the bathroom and he'd placed the order before she could change her mind again.

If he had Geordie's money, he'd never work on another kitchen newer than the nineteenth century. He didn't understand why she didn't see what talent she had. Why she didn't just tell her parents that she was going to be a photographer. Surely they'd be proud of her.

If he'd had parents . . .

GOING DOWN TOOK a little longer than the going up, but Geordie did it and when she stepped onto terra firma her knees held her up and she didn't feel sick. That was a start.

"Well, I've got to suit up and get back to work. See you girls later." Meri took off down the hall to the equipment room.

"Yeah, I know," Carlyn said. "Just being around her kind of keeps you going."

"I'll say. So can I help with anything this afternoon?"

"Nope, I'm off on an info-gathering trip to the archives. Doug should be back in an hour or so. You could see if Bruce needs anything."

"Right." Geordie followed Carlyn back to her office, picked up her camera bag and went to find Bruce. She was ambivalent about seeing him. He'd seen her at her most stupid, stuck on the scaffolding rails. He'd seen her at her most vulnerable, not when she was paralyzed with fear, but when he'd taken the time to look at her photographs. She knew then that he got what she was about. Because suddenly she could see her work through someone else's eyes. Someone whose judgment she could trust.

She hardly knew him, but she knew in that moment that he saw it, too. Still she wasn't ready to meet him face-to-face. It had been an interesting evening. One that could have turned out much differently, and she would have enjoyed it, probably, but she was glad it had turned out the way it had.

Now at least there wouldn't be that "next day" awkwardness. And if there was something that could develop between them, it would develop in its own time, in its own way.

He was standing at the sink, looking out the window.

"Hey," she said as she entered the kitchen.

"Hey." He turned but didn't meet her eyes. "You want coffee?"

"No . . . thanks. I need to apologize. I was trying to fake my way through this job instead of asking for help. And I screwed up."

He shrugged. He wasn't giving her much help. Maybe he was still angry, though last night he'd seemed anything but.

"Look I'm a spoiled rich kid. No, I was a spoiled rich kid. I'm an adult and I know it's about time I started acting like one."

"Like climbing up scaffolding when there's no one around if you fell?"

"It was stupid. I just wanted to—I had to prove something to myself and failed miserably. Anyway, thanks, for saving my butt. I would've still been up there if you hadn't come to the rescue." She sighed. "Seems like someone is always rescuing me."

"You're lucky."

"I know, and I'm appreciative. But when there is always someone to take care of you, send you money, bail you out when you get in over your head, it's not very conducive to standing on your own two feet and taking the consequences of your actions." She bit her lip. "And to have the courage of your convictions. Hell, I don't even have convictions. Or know what I want to do in life."

He quirked an eyebrow. A strange expression, and one that she couldn't read.

"I know, you think I'm an airhead. I am. It's just that I keep trying things and none of them last. I lose interest. And then I flake out." She lowered her eyes. "It's what I do."

He didn't say anything. She didn't know why she expected him too, but she could only look at her toes for so long. She looked up.

His head was cocked, his eyes crinkled as if he was amused. "Maybe you just never found the right thing for you."

She groaned. "I've tried. I tried journalism, I tried fashion photography, I tried gallery work, I tried . . ."

"Doesn't it occur to you that you've found the right thing but have been looking at the wrong part?"

"Huh?"

He crossed his arms and leaned back against the counter. The wrong part. What wrong part? And then she got it. In a moment of glorious epiphany. Hell, she wouldn't be surprised if a chorus of voices with full orchestra started singing like something from the karaoke bar.

Her camera. She was always looking outward, but seeing inward. That's what made her a good photographer. That's also what made her flit around like a total ass. Always looking out there for the perfect opportunity, when she'd been carrying it around with her all the time.

"What a dope I've been. I've just been dancing around on the fringes, afraid to make a real decision. One that would last my whole life, and get my family off my case. But I was looking for a quick fix. Dragging my camera around to all these different venues, when it wasn't out there, it was in the lens, in me.

"I don't have to find one thing and stick with it forever, because I have access to whatever I want, through the lens. I am such a dope."

"I wouldn't say that. Just stubborn."

"Carlyn said you all put piecemeal work together to keep doing this."

"It's the only way we get to do what we want to do."

"I can do that. Can't I?"

He shrugged.

She thought about it. She could photograph houses, people, landscapes, while she developed her own signature look, maybe have a gallery show—or two or ten. Open her own studio someday. For the first time ever, she could see a future, not all in one piece but developing sometimes quickly, sometimes slowly. Good times and bad times, hard and easy. But it could be hers. If she only had the courage to take the chance.

It was so obvious and so hokey that she almost laughed out loud.

Well, she'd start right now. She'd tell Carlyn that she'd like to rent the room in her apartment. And then she'd tell her dad.

"Bruce, you're amazing." She walked straight across the room and kissed him on the mouth. And that was pretty amazing, too. Then she turned and strode out the door.

"Me?" Bruce said, sounding stunned. "I didn't do anything."

She just waved and went to find Carlyn.

Geordie went straight home after work and spent the evening online, researching local photography businesses. She knew better than to strike out on her own right off the bat. Just look at Bruce. He at least had built a bit of a reputation so that he could supplement his restoration work with regular renovation.

She needed a steady job, one with a salary so she could budget and begin to save, so she could get her own place, and gradually build up a repertoire of gallery work. But not just any job. One that would challenge her, feed her creativity. It would be out there somewhere.

She typed in *photographic studios* and was surprised at how many there were in the area. She clicked on one at random, and the photos were just what she expected: weddings, anniversaries, family portraits. Most were nice, what most people wanted. A shot of bride and groom cutting cake, standing on the lawn with the sea in the background. Groups of posed shots, perfect for sending to relatives on Facebook and Pinterest, or framing on the office wall or over the piano. The kinds of photos that found their way to family albums, and recorded the day's events.

Perfectly respectable, perfect for what they were. But they were not for Geordie.

The old familiar flutter began in her stomach, turning to a knot. The renegade thoughts. This isn't going to work. Another dead end. I have to find something, have to start again. Have to . . . She wrote down the name and number, clicked on another and added it to the list.

She picked out a few and wrote down their e-mail addresses and phone numbers. She'd just get something for the present then try again later. Then she thought about standing behind a tripod, moving people closer together, standing and kneeling, so that everyone's face could be seen. Telling them to smile, counting to three. Never veering from the tried and true.

She tore off the list from her notepad and threw it in the trash.

She wouldn't settle for a job out of desperation, just to stop her parents from worrying about her, from pressuring her to settle down. She would find a happy medium, something that would be satisfying and would keep her solvent. Something that would give her time to work on her own photography but not sacrificing hours a day to work by the numbers or constantly scrambling for freelance work.

Her stomach growled. She went into the kitchen and got down the jar of peanut butter. Reached in the drawer for a spoon and touched the envelope she'd hidden the night before. it would be so easy just to take it, deposit it, and go on to the next chapter. Who was she kidding? Her life didn't have chapters, just thirty-second commercial spots.

She went back to her computer, kept at it. Found one studio that thought a little outside of the box. Used interesting filters, unusual backgrounds, an undirected moment. She could work like that.

The next one was a large studio but too traditional. The next more inventive, but just didn't speak to her. She skipped over some and lingered on others, rejected some and added others to her list, and by midnight she had a handful of A-list studios that spoke to her. Now if only her photographs spoke to them. And each was in need of a staff photographer.

She started to close the window, decided to look at just a few more. And found a real winner. Wedding portraits, anniversaries, head shots, they were all there. They were inventive, but they were more than that. They caught that internal spark of the people being photographed. They drew her in. She clicked through photo after photo, and thought, *Yeah, I could do that.*

She added the name and address to the top of the list. Glanced at the time. Eleven o'clock. Looked over to the photos lined up against the wall. She would have time to arrange a hard-copy portfolio as well as a digital one.

She closed out of the internet and opened her photo gallery.

Two hours later she had some definitive shots, ones she thought would appeal to the first studio on her list. She composed an e-mail, mentioned how their photos had drawn her in. Attached a few of her own. Asked for a job.

Six e-mails later, her eyes began to close and she caught herself making spelling mistakes. Six was a good start. She'd do more tomorrow.

And if no one answered, she would go in person, take her portfolio, keep her fingers crossed that they would give her a job.

No, not a job, a career.

Chapter 12

. . . .

GEORDIE DIDN'T TELL anyone what she'd done, not her colleagues and not her parents. Days passed. She got two no-thank-yous, but mainly just no responses. That was the problem with e-mail, you never knew if they just weren't interested, if the e-mail had gone to their spam folder, or if they were so busy they hadn't gotten to it yet.

Each night she went home to check her e-mail and send out more. Each night she picked up the envelope, put it down again. She had to get off this treadmill, even if she had to go crawling back to her family later. At least she had a family to crawl back to.

She thought about Bruce, virtually alone in the world, who took the leap to go it alone. Doug, whose accident had taken away his profession; he'd created another one for himself, but it couldn't have been easy. Meri and Carlyn loved their work, even though they had to pinch pennies all the time. Carlyn could make a lot more money doing something else, but she chose not to. And Meri? She had never thought of doing something else.

And Geordie wanted to be like that. She was like that. Maybe that's why she'd never settled down: if something didn't look feasible immediately, she panicked and tried something else.

Yeah, she had a short attention span, but not when she was photographing. Then she could work for hours without stopping. Could go back day after day. It was something she wanted to go back to day after day. And if she had to piece together several part-time jobs to do it, she would. She had saved the four hundred dollars to rent Carlyn's extra room; she could live like everyone else.

What would she miss about her life? This apartment? She'd never felt at home here. It wasn't home. And since she'd started work at the Gilbert House, she hadn't even thought about going to a fancy restaurant, a trendy bar, or a quick trip to any resort. Didn't miss them. She'd had fun at the local karaoke bar.

She took a breath.

It was time.

She walked over to the kitchen counter, opened the drawer. Picked up the envelope. Opened it, slid the check out. One thing about her dad, he was generous. She could take it to the bank, cash it, it would give her a little pad until she got established—just one more time.

And that's what always got her in trouble, the just one more time. She took a breath, slowly tore the check across the center and again, and again, until little pieces rained into the wastepaper basket.

Then she sat down at her computer and opened her e-mail.

Dear Dad, Received your check. I really appreciate it as always, but I've decided not to cash it. It's time I did things for myself. I'll be sharing an apartment with a colleague until I can afford a place of my own. I love photography and I'll figure out how to make a living doing it. I hope you'll be happy with my decision. Love, Geordie.

She read it over. And pressed SEND.

There it was done. She went back to her job search.

Her phone rang. Surely her father couldn't have read the e-mail already.

She picked it up.

"Ms. Holt?"

"Yes?"

"This is Roger Diffens of Diffens Photography. I've looked over your portfolio, and I wondered if you'd be interested in coming down to discuss doing some work for us . . ."

SHE HUNG UP. She had an in-person interview. He liked her work. Thought she might be a good fit. Could she come in the next day? She told him she could get there during lunch.

Diffens was one of her first-choice studios. She practically danced across the room to her line of photos. Chose a couple of portraits and carefully lifted them off their backing. Got out her portfolio and chose a few more. Then back to the computer, where she began to print several others.

She had no illusions about how easy or hard the life she'd chosen would be. But for the first time in her life, she was really ready to face it. And she owed a lot of that realization to her colleagues at Gilbert House.

A half hour passed and she was totally involved with organizing her portfolio.

Her phone rang.

This would be her father.

Hello?"

Silence.

"Hello?"

"Hey. It's Bruce. I was thinking about coming down near you for a bite to eat. And thought maybe if you hadn't eaten, you might want to come. I know a place that has dynamite burgers. If you're not busy."

"I'm busy, but I'd love to."

"You sound different. Is everything okay?"

"Yep. In a nutshell, I tore up my allowance, e-mailed my father that I was giving up money and apartment and striking out on my own. I must be nuts. But then Roger Diffens, this really good photographer called and I have an interview with him tomorrow. Is that amazing, or what?"

"Amazing. That's really great."

"Yeah. Kind of scary."

"You'll be okay. Might be tough at first, but if it's important, it will be worth the effort."

"I know. I have a good feeling about this. A different feeling. A really scared but happy feeling." She smiled. *A really happy feeling.* "I'm just putting some photos together, but I'm starving."

"A half hour okay?"

"Perfect."

"Uh, it's nothing fancy. See you then." He hung up.

Amazing. A job interview and a . . . a date? She automatically went to her closet and started looking through her clothes. Stopped. Looked down at her jeans—not her best, and kind of beat up from work. Kind of perfect for her new life.

She did wash her face and put on makeup. No reason to go totally overboard.

When the intercom buzzed she was ready.

Bruce stood at the door, still dressed in his work clothes, a champagne bottle in his hand. A fairly good champagne, too.

"What's that for?"

"We're celebrating." He held up the bottle. "Not as good as the one you have in the fridge but pretty nice."

It was, and he shouldn't have spent the money on her . . . on them?

He poured the champagne and handed her a glass. "Congratulations on your new career, your new job, your new . . ."

"Attitude."

They touched glasses. Took a sip.

"This is pretty good," she said.

He grinned. "Well, drink up. From here on out it's going to be beer on tap."

Beer on tap. Hmm. It sounded like a pretty good way to go.

Want more?
See what happens next in Shelley
Noble's stunning novel

Breakwater Bay

Prologue

· · · · · · · · ·

ALDEN WASN'T SUPPOSED to take the dinghy out today. That's the last thing his dad said when he left for work that morning. "Don't go on the water. There's a bad storm brewing."

He'd only meant to be out long enough to catch something for dinner, but the storm had come in too fast. Now the water boiled black around him. Already he could hardly tell the difference between the black clouds overhead and the black rocks of the breakwater. Knives of rain slashed at his eyes and slapped his windbreaker against his skin. The shore looked so far away. He knew where the tide would pull him before he got there.

He was scared. His dad would kill him if he wrecked the dinghy. A huge wave crashed over the boat, throwing him to the floor. One oar was snatched from his hand and he barely managed to grab it before it slipped from the lock. And he forgot all about what punishment he would get and prayed he could stay alive to receive it.

He threw himself onto the bench and started rowing as hard as he could.

And then he saw her. A dark form. Standing on the rocks. At first he thought she must be a witch conjured from the storm. He tried to wipe his eyes on his sleeve, but he couldn't let go of the oars.

She waved her hands and began to scramble down the rocks. And then she slipped and disappeared.

He stopped trying to save himself and let the break-water draw the boat in. He knew just when to stick out the oar to keep from crashing. Held on with all his strength. The dinghy crunched as it hit, and he flung the rope over the spike his dad had hammered into the rock years before.

He couldn't see her now. He clambered from the boat, slipped on the rocks. Called out, but the wind snatched his voice away.

And suddenly there she was, lying not three feet away. Motionless.

He crawled over the slimy rocks, grabbing at whatever would keep him from sliding back into the sea, and knelt beside her; shook her. "Lady? Lady, you gotta get up."

She didn't move.

"Lady. Please. You gotta get up." He pulled on her arm, but she only turned over. She wasn't a lady. She was just a girl. Wearing jeans. Not that much older than him.

He grabbed under her shoulders and tried to drag her

toward the boat. She was heavy, heavier than she looked, and she wouldn't help.

And he just kept thinking, *Please don't be dead.*

Then she moved. Her eyes opened, and they were wide and scared. She grabbed hold of him, nearly knocking him over, but together they crawled to where the dinghy bucked like a bronco in the waves.

He didn't know how he got her into the boat, or how he rowed to shore, or pushed the dinghy to safety on the rocky beach. He was so cold he couldn't feel his fingers or his feet. And she'd closed her eyes again. This time he didn't try to wake her; he ran, not home, but across the dunes to Calder Farm. Burst into their kitchen and fell to his knees.

"The beach. Help her." And everything went black.

When he awoke he was lying in a bed, covered in heavy quilts.

"Go back to sleep. Everything's all right."

Gran Calder.

"Is she dead?"

She patted the quilt by his shoulder. "No, no. You saved her life. You were very brave."

His lip began to tremble. He couldn't stop it.

Then somebody screamed and she hurried out of the room. He pulled the covers over his head so he wouldn't hear, but he couldn't breathe. Another scream, worse than before. What were they doing to her?

He slid out from the covers but he wasn't wearing anything. Someone had taken his clothes. He pulled the quilt from the bed, wrapped it around himself and dragged it out into the hallway.

Only one light was on, but a door was ajar at the end of the hall. He crept toward it, trailing the quilt behind him.

The girl screamed again. Then stopped.

He stopped, too, frightened even more by that sudden silence.

Then a new, smaller cry filled the air.

Chapter 1

· · · · · · · · · ·

MERI HOLLIS DROPPED the paint chip into a manila envelope and rolled from her back to sit upright on the scaffolding.

She stretched her legs along the rough wood and cracked her neck. It had been a long day, first standing, then sitting, then lying on her back. Every muscle protested as she leaned forward to touch her toes, but she knew better than to start the descent before her circulation was going again.

While she waited, she labeled the newest sample, added it to the file box and placed it in a bucket, which she lowered thirty feet to the floor. She flipped off her head lamp, pulled it from her head, and took a last look at her little corner of the world, which in the dim light looked just as sooty and faded as it had twenty hours, two hundred paint samples and several gallons of vinegar and water ago.

It had been slow going. The meticulous cleaning of paint

layers was never fast, even on a flat ceiling, but when you added plaster ornamentation, extreme care was needed. But she had finally reached enough of the original ceiling that she was sure it had been painted in the mid eighteen hundreds.

It was exciting. Especially if what she suspected turned out to be true.

She'd discovered the first fleck of gold that afternoon. Surely there would be more. But further study would have to wait until Monday. She was calling it a day.

She stored her tools and slowly lowered one foot to the first rung of the pipe ladder that would take her to the ground floor. Work had stopped in the grand foyer a half hour ago, but she'd been determined to finish that one test section today.

She reached the bottom on creaky ankles and knees. Grabbed hold of the ladder and stretched her calves and thighs. Then she picked up her file box and tools and carried them to the workroom.

Carlyn Anderson looked up from where she was logging in data from the day's work. "You're the last one."

Meri deposited her file on the table and arched her back. "Now I know how Michelangelo felt. Only he ended up with the Sistine Chapel and I got a sooty ceiling in a minor mansion with two hundred-plus chips from twenty layers of ancient paint in various hues of ick."

"Yeah, but just imagine what it will look like when it's back in its original state."

"Actually I got a glimpse of it today. If I'm not mistaken, there's gold in them thar hills."

"Gilt?"

"Maybe. It might be a composite. In the state the ceiling's in, it's impossible to tell without the microscope." Meri pulled a stool over to the table and sat down. "Why the hell would anyone paint over a decorative ceiling from the nineteenth century?"

"The same reason they painted over the Owen Jones wallpaper with psychedelic orange."

"Oh well, someone's bad taste is our job security," Meri said. "Is there someone left who can take this over to the lab tonight?" She handed Carlyn the manila envelope of samples.

"I will, but you owe me, since you've blown off karaoke tomorrow night. And it's Sixties Night." Carlyn went through several doo-wop moves they'd been practicing on their lunch hour.

"Sorry, but I promised Gran I'd come out for my birthday dinner tonight. I'm not looking forward to a forty-minute ride but I couldn't say no. And tomorrow I'm having my birthday dinner with Peter." She yawned.

"You don't sound too excited."

"Well, I did turn thirty today somewhere between layer four—baby-poop brown—and layer three—seventies-kitchen green."

"You're in your prime."

"I'm slipping into middle age and instead of getting a proposal, Peter decides to go back to law school." Meri slid off the stool.

"Maybe he'll propose before then. Maybe tomorrow night."

"Maybe, but I'm not holding my breath. Don't listen to me. I'm just tired. I've got a great job, great friends, a family who loves me and . . ." Meri grinned at Carlyn. "Karaoke. Now, I'd better get going if I want to get a shower in before I hit the road."

"Well, happy birthday."

"Thanks."

"Oh, Doug wants to see you in his office before you go."

Meri winced. "We can guess he's not giving me a raise?"

"No but he should kiss your butt for the extra hours you're putting in gratis."

Meri yawned. "I'd rather have a raise."

"I'll walk you down."

Meri picked up her coat and bag from her locker and the two of them headed back to the kitchen, also known as Doug's office, to see what the project manager could possibly want on a Friday night.

The door swung inward, but the kitchen was dark.

"Are you sure he's still here?" Meri asked, groping for the light switch.

The lights came on. "Surprise!"

Beside her, Carlyn guffawed. "I can't believe you didn't know what was going on."

Meri laughed. "You guys."

Carlyn pushed her into the center of the room where at least twelve architectural restoration workers stood around the kitchen table and a large sheet cake with a huge number of candles.

Doug Paxton came over to give Meri a hug. He was a big,

brawny guy who had been relegated to ground work after falling through the floor of an abandoned house and breaking both legs and a hip five years before. He'd grown a little soft around the middle but he still exuded power and good taste. And he knew his way around a restoration better than anybody she knew.

"Happy birthday. Now come blow out your candles."

Someone had lit the candles during the hug and the cake was ablaze.

"I may need help," Meri said. "And these better not be trick candles." Though she didn't really know what to wish for. She had everything she wanted, a good job, great friends, a loving family, everything else except a fiancé. She was in no hurry, even if she *was* thirty. So she wished that life would stay good and that things would eventually work out for Peter and her and that the project would find the funding it would need for a complete restoration.

"What are you waiting for? Hurry up. The candles are about to gut."

Meri took a deep breath, motioned to everybody to help and the candles were extinguished. Cake was cut, seltzer was brought out, since Doug didn't allow any alcohol on a site, and a good time was had by all, for nearly a half an hour until Meri made her apologies and headed for her apartment, a shower and a long drive out to the farm.

TRAFFIC WAS HEAVY as Meri drove north out of Newport. Gran lived about a fifteen-minute stone's throw across the bay. But to drive there she had to go up to Portsmouth, across the bridge, then south again. So she hunkered down to endure the cars, the dark, and the rain.

It must have been raining all day, not that she'd noticed, because the streets and sidewalks were slick and puddles had formed in the uneven asphalt. She never did notice things when she was deep into a project. She had great powers of concentration and could spend hours lost in the zone.

Even as a child, Meri would look up from reading, or weeding, or just lying in the sea grass thinking, to find her three brothers standing over her. "We've been calling you for hours," they'd complain. "Dinner's ready." And they'd drag her to her feet and race her across the dunes to the house they shared with Gran. When Meri was fifteen her father was granted a research position at Yale and the family moved to New Haven, only seeing Gran on long weekends and holidays.

Meri sighed. Thirty must be the age when you started reminiscing about life. She was definitely feeling nostalgic tonight. Maybe it was because her future was suddenly looking a little hazy. Though she had to admit, Peter's change of plans hadn't thrown her into depths of despair. After her initial shock and dismay, her first thought was she would have more time to concentrate on her work without feeling guilty about neglecting him.

Obviously, neither of them was ready for total commitment. This would give them some time to really figure things out.

As she crossed the bridge at Tiverton, the drizzle became

a deluge, and her little hatchback was buffeted by gusts of wind that didn't let up until she turned south again toward Calder Farm. She could see the house across the dunes long before she got there. Every window was lit and the clapboard and stone farmhouse shone like a lighthouse out of the dark. Way to the left of it, Alden Corrigan's monstrous old house appeared as an ominous shadow.

Meri smiled. Looks could be deceiving. Alden's house was merely untended. It had seen its share of unhappiness like most of the old houses in the area, but it had also had its share of good times.

Meri turned into the car path and bumped slowly toward the house. Most of the menagerie of animals that found their way to the farm had probably taken shelter in the barn at the first sign of rain. Still Meri peered through the dark for moving forms and gleaming eyes until she came to a stop at the front of the house.

A silver Mercedes was parked outside. Meri grabbed her overnight bag from the backseat, ducked into the rain and dashed toward the kitchen door, which opened just as she got there, casting a bright spotlight on her as she rushed inside.

"Hi, Gran." Meri kissed her cheek and shrugged out of her dripping jacket. "What smells so good?"

Gran took her coat. "Your favorite, as if you didn't know. Now come inside."

Meri stepped into the kitchen, shaking the rain off. A man got up from the table. He was tall with hair combed back from a high forehead, and smile lines creasing his eyes and mouth.

"Dad!" Meri said. She dropped her case and purse and gave him a wet hug. "I can't believe you're here. Why didn't you tell me you were coming? Is that a new car?"

He laughed and pushed her gently to arm's length, then planted a kiss on her forehead. "I wasn't sure I could get away. Happy birthday."

Gran gave her a pat. "Go wash up and we'll eat."

Meri hurried to the powder room, followed by several cats that appeared from nowhere for the sole purpose of trying to trip her up on her way down the hall.

Daniel Hollis had married Meri's mother when Meri was three; three sons came at regular intervals after that and every spare space was put to use as the Hollis family grew.

Now Gran lived mostly downstairs. She was still young—only seventy-five or so, she told everyone—but since she lived alone they'd all made her promise not to go up and down the stairs, a promise that she promptly broke. As she explained when Meri caught her vacuuming the bedroom carpets, "I can't live comfortably knowing all that dust is gathering above my head."

When Meri returned to the kitchen, there were bowls of steaming cioppino set at three places, and the aroma of the rich seafood stew filled the air. They'd just sat down, when there was a knock at the door.

"Come in, Alden," Gran called from the table. "That man could smell cioppino from the next county."

The door opened and "that man," a tall, ridiculously thin, broodingly handsome forty-two-year-old man ducked in the low door and stood dripping on the flagstone floor.

"Get yourself a bowl and sit down," Gran said.

"Thanks, but I can't stay. I just came to say happy birthday."

Gran gave him a look that Meri didn't understand and Alden chose to ignore. He walked over to Meri and before she could even stand, he dropped a flat giftwrapped package on the table. "Happy birthday."

"Thanks. Can't you stay? I haven't seen you in forever."

"I know, but I have a bunch of work to get finished and I'm way behind. You staying for the weekend?"

"Just till tomorrow."

"Then I'll see you before you leave."

"At least wait until I open your present."

She pulled at the string that was tied around the package; the bow released and with it the paper.

"I couldn't find the tape," he said.

"Why am I not surprised?" She lifted out a piece of cardboard where a pen and ink drawing had been mounted. It was a girl, her hair curling down her back, sitting on the rocks gazing out to sea. The rocks of the breakwater on the beach between the two houses. It looked like her.

"It's beautiful, Alden. Thank you. Is it Ondine?" she asked, teasing him. Taciturn and reclusive, he was best known for his illustrations of children's books.

"Good God, no."

"Oh," she said, surprised at his reaction. "Who then?"

"Just someone sitting on the rocks."

"Ah. Well, I love it. Thank you. I'm going to have it framed and put it on my living-room wall in Newport."

"I'd better be going, your dinner is getting cold."

"You're sure you don't want—"

"Can't," Alden said. "But happy birthday. Dan. Gran."

Gran shook her finger at him. But he was gone.

"Well, that was weird," Meri said.

His leaving seemed to cast a pall over the room.

"Let's eat," Gran said.

Meri dug in, but she noticed that Gran merely picked at her food. Dan seemed to have lost his appetite, too. Meri didn't understand. The stew was heavenly, but their lack of enthusiasm was catching and she pushed her bowl away before it was empty.

"Delicious," she said with a satisfied sigh, though it was a little forced.

The atmosphere had definitely taken a plunge since Alden's visit. She wanted to know why. "Is something happening with Alden? Why didn't he stay for dinner?"

"Oh you know Alden," Gran said and began clearing the table.

She *did* know Alden. They'd grown up together, sort of. He was already a teenager when she was born and by the time she was old enough to pester him and follow him around, he was in high school.

Gran refused help with the dishes and Meri and her father traded work stories until Gran returned with a homemade carrot raisin cake and one big candle. "I always keep a box of birthday candles," Gran explained. "But I guess they melted in last summer's heat wave. So you only get one."

"That's fine," Meri told her. "It will make up for the forest of candles on the cake at work."

They ate cake and Gran pulled a festively wrapped package from the shopping bag she'd placed by the side of her chair.

Meri opened it slowly and neatly, a trait that she was born with and was a big plus in her chosen profession, but sometimes made her brothers scream, "Just tear off the paper."

"How are the three Musketeers? Are Gabe and Penny all set for the baby?"

"Oh yeah, for months now." Dan sighed and Meri knew he was thinking about her mother, who had died only four years before. She would never see any of her grandchildren.

"Let's see. Matt just got a raise and Will is having way too much fun at Georgetown."

"Oh yeah, I got e-cards from both of them yesterday. And Penny sent a lovely card and signed both Gabe and her names."

The paper came off and Meri opened the box. It contained a hand-knitted pullover sweater in Meri's favorite colors of blue, lavender and burgundy. "It's gorgeous. Did May McAllister knit this?"

"Yes, she did. And she said if it didn't fit just right to bring it by the store and she'd fix it."

"Everything she's ever made has fit perfectly," Meri said. "Thank you so much."

Gran smiled.

Dan stood and pulled a jeweler's box out of his pants pocket. He walked over to Meri and handed it to her, then stood beside her as she opened it. It was a locket of brushed gold. The inside held two tiny pictures, one of her mother and one of Dan.

Sudden tears sprang to Meri's eyes. "Thank you. It's beautiful."

He hugged her. "You're the most precious thing in the world to me and to your mother, too."

Meri smiled up at him as he clasped the necklace around her neck. She was so lucky that this man had come into their lives and taken them both into his heart. He'd been more than a stepdad; her real father couldn't have loved her more.

Meri had noticed a cardboard box, a little larger than a shoe box, sitting on the antique kitchen hutch. Just an ordinary cardboard box that might be sent through the mail, though this one was dented and smashed from years of storage.

Now Gran went to the hutch, but instead of retrieving the box, she took an envelope from the top and brought it to the table, where she placed it in front of Meri.

"Another present?" Meri asked.

Her father's lips tightened. "Not exactly a present," he said.

"More like a confession," Gran said and Meri swore there were tears in her eyes.

About the Author

· · · · · · · · · ·

SHELLEY NOBLE is a former professional dancer and choreographer. She most recently worked on the films *Mona Lisa Smile* and *The Game Plan*. She is a member of Sisters in Crime, Mystery Writers of America, and Romance Writers of America.

www.shelleynoble.com

Visit www.AuthorTracker.com for exclusive information on your favorite HarperCollins authors.